INCREDIBLES 2

A REAL STRETCH

Design by Winnie Ho and Susan Gerber

For information address Disney Press, 1200 Grand Central Avenue, Glendale, California 91201.

Printed in the United States of America

First Hardcover Edition, May 2018
10 9 8 7 6 5 4 3 2 1

FAC-020093-18086

Library of Congress Control Number: 2017961267

ISBN 978-1-368-01192-1

Visit disneybooks.com

THIS LABEL APPLIES TO TEXT STOCK

Disney · PIXAR

INCREDIBLES 2

A REAL STRETCH

AN *Elastigirl* PREQUEL STORY

By **Carla Jablonksi**

Disney PRESS
LOS ANGELES • NEW YORK

CHAPTER 1

C*RASH!*

Elastigirl's head whipped around at the sound of breaking glass. She shot quick glances up and down the street. It had been a very quiet morning for the Super on patrol in Municiberg.

Till now.

She heard a shout come from around the corner. Using her very special Super power, Elastigirl stretched . . . and stretched . . . and *stretched* her neck. She popped her head around the edge of the building to take a quick look.

She spotted the culprit immediately: a man dressed all in black with a very obvious bald spot on the back of his head. He was leaping into an open convertible, one hand brandishing a collection of jewels, a long pearl necklace dangling between his fingers. The broken jewelry store window told her the rest of the story.

Could it be? Could this thief be none other than Mysterious Melvin, the criminal mastermind who had been responsible for a spate of jewelry store break-ins?

Elastigirl knew exactly how to find out. She stretched her arm all the way to the store and wiggled it through the broken window, taking care to avoid the sharp shards of glass. She picked up the piece of fancy stationery left on a pedestal that had just moments before held thousands of dollars' worth of jewelry. She retracted her arm and read the note.

Yep. Mysterious Melvin was at it again. So far the thief had eluded police. They hadn't been able to pinch him yet, and the police were pretty annoyed. Moreover, the criminal taunted them after each burglary, leaving a note at the crime scene that read: *What's yours is mine! Ha ha! –M. M.*

There were rumors that he had once been an escape artist with a vaudeville sideshow. Others said he'd had a failed career on the stage. What everyone agreed on was that he was daring and inventive and no one knew what he looked like. A master of disguise, not only did Mysterious Melvin completely change his appearance for each crime, but he never used the same escape method twice. That made him very difficult to apprehend unless he was caught in the act. Like now.

Suddenly, the crime alert signal Elastigirl wore pinned to her headband went off, *ding-ding-ding*ing and flashing red. She tapped the button and shouted, "I'm on it!" letting the other Supers and the National Supers Agency know she was in pursuit of the perp.

Melvin's car kicked into high gear—and so did Elastigirl. She raced after the speeding vehicle.

"Come on, feet," she urged, pushing herself hard to catch up. But Mysterious Melvin had a head start, and he careened through the streets in clever evasive moves.

I need more speed! Elastigirl thought, not for the first time. Even though she was stretching her legs to capacity—the length of two city blocks—Melvin was getting away!

She spotted a group of motorcycle enthusiasts hanging out in front of a soda shop a few blocks ahead of her. *R-e-a-c-h-i-n-g* out with a super-stretched arm, she tapped one of the riders just as he was about to mount his bike. She grabbed the handlebars with her other hand. "Hey, fella!" she hollered, her head still a full street away. "Can I borrow this?"

Startled, the guy whipped around, stumbling away from the motorcycle. When he saw whom those spaghettilike arms belonged to, a wide grin spread on his face.

"Anything for you, Elastigirl!" he shouted.

Elastigirl snapped her arms back to their normal length, yanking the powerful bike underneath her. She revved the engines and took off with a *vrrrrooooom*!

"Go get him, Elastigirl!"

"You're swell!"

"Yay, Elastigirl!"

The cheering was nearly drowned out as the motorcycle roared past the group. She hunkered down low, feeling the rumble of the bike vibrate through her. Peering through her red mask, she set her sights on the rapidly vanishing vehicle up ahead. Tires squealed as the reckless driver made one sharp turn after another.

She charged after the speeding convertible with a roar. She wove in and out of traffic, always keeping her brown eyes trained on her quarry. The motorcycle was faster than her feet, but not as fast as that souped-up car.

Maybe she could grab Mysterious Melvin's steering wheel and control the car from the motorcycle. Or somehow stomp the car's brakes.

She gripped the sides of the motorcycle tightly with her legs. Releasing first one arm, then the other, she steadied herself hands-free on the back of the speeding bike. She stretched out her arms.

"Whoa!" Elastigirl let out a yelp as the motorcycle swerved and dipped. She yanked back her arms. *Jeepers!* Having her arms all the way out like that messed with her balance on the bike.

She revved the motor, but the bike was already moving at top speed. She decided to try reaching out to step on the convertible's brakes. If she stretched only one leg, maybe she'd still be able to control the bike.

Leaning a bit to one side to compensate for the shift in her weight distribution, she stretched out a leg: longer . . . longer . . . longer . . .

Melvin sped around a corner.

Elastigirl gnashed her teeth as she retracted her leg. To make that turn she'd have to be sitting squarely on the bike. If only the motorcycle could stretch along with her. If that had been possible, she'd have caught Mysterious Melvin by now.

"Come on, come on, come *on*!" She gripped the handlebars tightly as she swooped around the corner, her red gloves stretched across her knuckles. She was *not* going to let Melvin get away with this robbery. Not going to let him laugh at the police department again. *No, sir!*

"What's happening up there . . . ?" Elastigirl murmured, frowning as the traffic in front of her came to a standstill.

She zipped her motorcycle between the stopped cars and trucks. "Yes!" she cheered when she spotted the cause of the slowdown. An over-turned garbage truck. Right in front of Mysterious Melvin's convertible.

Mysterious Melvin may have had a head start,

but Elastigirl was the one with the luck—not to mention the Super powers!

Elastigirl leapt off the motorcycle. She stretched her legs to the max and picked her way through the cars and the toppled garbage bags toward Mysterious Melvin's hemmed-in convertible.

Her nose wrinkled as she neared the garbage truck. *Sheesh! What a smell!* Even high above the street, the stench was nearly overpowering. The whole area was strewn with fish bones, wet newspapers, dirty diapers, old tissues, and other trash that Elastigirl really didn't care to identify.

Melvin was banging the steering wheel in frustration. "Get out of the way!" he shouted. When Elastigirl's super-tall shadow loomed over him, he glanced up. Elastigirl noticed he was wearing a very intricate mask made of little mirrors that reflected his surroundings, including the sparkly loot resting on the seat beside him.

"No!" Mysterious Melvin scrambled to undo his seat belt.

"Sorry, Melvin," Elastigirl said. "What's yours is mine." She reached into the open car and yanked him out with one hand, then grabbed the handful of jewels with the other. On her stretched legs, she towered over the stalled vehicles and gaping pedestrians. She looked around, trying to figure out what to do with the thief.

"Ah!" Stepping over the stopped cars, she dumped Mysterious Melvin into the back of the garbage truck. "It's time to take out the trash," she quipped.

Whoooooosh!

Elastigirl turned to see a sheet of ice forming a path leading directly toward her. She knew what that meant.

"Frozone," she said in greeting to her pal and fellow Super.

Frozone slid up with a flurry of ice shavings as he came to a stop. "Elastigirl. What do we have here?" Slim and sleek, Frozone radiated cool. And it wasn't just because of his power to harness water molecules in the air to send ice blasts, create slick frozen pathways, and turn villains into Popsicles.

"One master thief, apprehended," Elastigirl announced proudly. "The cops can take it from here." Elastigirl waved over the police officers who hovered nearby. Once they'd approached, she tossed the jewels to one officer while the other quickly handcuffed and unmasked Mysterious Melvin.

"You beat us all here," Frozone said as the police officers hauled the thief away. "You're one super Super."

"I was nearby." Elastigirl dismissed the compliment as she rearranged the headband in her red hair.

Frozone's nose crinkled under his goggles. "If that's your current perfume, I suggest you find another brand."

Elastigirl laughed. "It's called eau de gar-bahge."

Car horns started honking around them. Elastigirl sighed, pulling up her gloves and smoothing out the wrinkles. "I better get these cars back on the road. Otherwise, we'll have to break up some angry motorists."

"True, true."

As if on cue, two drivers started shouting and gesturing angrily, each claiming right of way. Elastigirl turned toward them, but Frozone held up a gloved hand. "I'll take care of them. I believe they need some *cooling off*." He gave her a wink, then jogged to the end of the street and stepped in between the irritated drivers.

"From catching criminals to directing traffic." Elastigirl sighed as she studied the tangle of cars, vans, and trucks in front of her. "All in a day's work, I guess."

Suddenly, a large masked man rounded the corner. He strode decisively to the garbage truck sitting in the middle of the street and lifted it over his head. Without even breaking a sweat or showing any strain, he turned this way and that, obviously searching for a place to put it.

"Hey!" The terrified driver hung his head out the window. "What are you doing? Put us down!" Another man nervously peeked out from the passenger side.

"The workers are still inside the truck!" Elastigirl called to the newcomer.

The Super looked at Elastigirl quizzically, then craned his neck to see the driver above him.

"Don't worry, my friends," the supersized Super said. "Just clearing the way. Hang on." Then he addressed the people in the cars and trucks around him. "Okay, on your way. Slowly," he added as two cars started their engines at the same time. In just a few minutes, the vehicles were moving along in an orderly fashion again.

Grinning at Elastigirl, the brawny Super carried the garbage truck to the curb and gently set it down in front of her. Elastigirl could see the driver wiping the sweat from his face with a handkerchief, his partner laughing nervously. The driver took a deep breath and started up the truck.

"Impressed?" the masked Super asked Elastigirl as the garbage truck drove away. He towered over her.

Elastigirl rolled her eyes. *I was until you asked me that question,* she thought.

Before she could reply, Frozone slid toward them. "My two favorite people!" He slung an arm over Elastigirl's shoulder and shook hands with the conceited Super. "Elastigirl, this is Mr. Incredible. Recently returned from a special assignment."

Elastigirl eyed the grinning man with more interest now. She took in the blond cowlick curling over his forehead, the blue eyes twinkling through the mask, the prominent chin. His Supersuit was blue and black with a big letter *I* in the center of the chest. "So you're Incredible," Elastigirl said. She'd heard a lot about him, mostly from Frozone.

"Some say so," Mr. Incredible said, with false modesty.

Ego much? Elastigirl wasn't sure how to respond aloud, so instead she turned to Frozone. "See ya later. I've got a motorcycle to return." Giving Mr. Incredible a sharp nod as a goodbye, she spun around and headed toward the bike she had discarded.

"Why is she so *bent out of shape*?" Mr. Incredible joked behind her.

Elastigirl heard Frozone groan at the bad pun as she mounted the motorcycle. Then she tore away.

Now that she wasn't chasing down a criminal, Elastigirl could let herself enjoy the ride. She leaned low over the handlebars, reveling in the connection she had to the powerful machine. Even the tiniest move she made had an effect as she thundered along the street. The breeze against her face was nice and cool, and the air smelled of water from the nearby wharf. If she had been able to stretch the bike, she could've seen the band shell on the pier a few blocks away.

I wonder if it would be possible to make a bike that could change shape and size, Elastigirl thought.

She stopped to allow a group of schoolchildren to cross the street in front of her. "We're going to the zoo!" a little boy exclaimed.

"That sounds like fun," she told him.

She glanced up at the zoo's entrance in front of her. It was festooned with balloons and enormous posters announcing the latest exhibits. She really should get there soon, she thought. According to a newspaper article she'd read that morning, there was a brand-new tiger everyone very excited about. She'd love to see the majestic animal.

After the children passed, Elastigirl revved the engine. She spotted the motorcycle enthusiasts still chatting in front of the soda shop, including the burly bearded guy she'd borrowed the bike from. She popped wheelies in front of the group, who all cheered and clapped.

"Thanks for the loan," Elastigirl said to the bike's owner as she hopped off.

"How could I say no to Elastigirl?" he replied, a big grin spreading across his bearded face. "It's an honor to think that not only did you ride my bike, you used it to catch a criminal."

"You looked like a natural," a young woman wearing a helmet with purple racing stripes said. "You should get one of these."

"I'm thinking about it," Elastigirl said.

"I'm Adam, and this is Judy," the bike's owner said. "Wow. I'm amazed to be even talking to you."

"Yeah," Judy added. "We really are big fans. What you do for Municiberg. For all of us. Well, it's hard to know how to thank you."

"But–thank you," Adam said.

Elastigirl wasn't really sure how to respond to all the gratitude. She was a Super. It was a *given* that she would use her powers to help, to keep Municiberg safe. She was doing her duty, doing what she was born to do–not to mention being paid by the National Supers Agency. But for her it wasn't just a job; it was her life's calling. She didn't expect people to thank her for doing what she knew she was meant to do.

"Well, um, glad to be of service," she finally

said. "And thank *you*. That motorcycle was a big help. And a cool transport."

The bearded man climbed onto his motorcycle. "You got that right. I've had this baby for about ten years now. Keep it in mint condition. I take care of it, it takes care of me."

Elastigirl respected the attention and pride he took with the machine. Cars, tools, devices—they all required proper maintenance. Even though it was a small thing, Elastigirl made sure her crime alert signal was in good working order every day. If that failed, she might miss an emergency call and let the good citizens of Municiberg down. And she wasn't going to let that happen.

After thanking the man one more time, Elastigirl headed off, imagining what it would feel like to be riding instead of walking. *Maybe one day . . .*

CHAPTER 2

"Good work today, Elastigirl," Agent Rick Dicker said.

"Happy to be of service," Elastigirl replied. She tipped back in her chair and propped her booted feet on Dicker's desk, crossing her legs at the ankles.

They sat in Dicker's office at the National Supers Agency in downtown Municiberg. Although the agency headquarters were state of the art, with labs, a training facility sporting the most current fitness equipment, and wood-paneled conference rooms, Rick Dicker's office had a more old-fashioned, run-down feel. A creaky fan whirred on top of a dusty file cabinet that was so full the drawers didn't quite shut. Bits of files and papers peeked out of the crammed cabinet. The wall behind his desk was covered with frames: photos of Dicker and various Supers at special events, newspaper clippings, thank-you letters from citizens, and fan mail from children.

The door flew open and Dicker's secretary, Shirley, strode in. Elastigirl was always curious about what Shirley would be wearing; her outfits were usually pretty outrageous. This one was no exception: bright purple stirrup pants, pink sandals, and an orange tunic with yellow swirls. Her mass of frizzy gray hair was piled high on top of her head. She was quite the contrast to her boss and his uniform of drab brown suits. "Here are those briefs you wanted, sir," she told Dicker as she put some files on his desk. "Elastigirl, can I get you anything? Coffee? Tea?"

"I'm all right. Thanks, Shirley," Elastigirl replied.

"You betcha," she said. "Well, if that's all, I've got some work to do."

"Oh, yes, thank you, Shirley," Dicker said.

The colorful secretary nodded, then made her way to the door.

"So, what's on your mind?" Elastigirl asked her

NSA point person once Shirley was gone. "I don't think you called me in here just to praise me for bringing in Mysterious Melvin. I've caught plenty of criminals since joining the NSA."

Dicker took off his glasses and cleaned them with a handkerchief. "You know me too well," he commented.

"Well, we do go back a ways," Elastigirl said. Funny. She had been just a teenager when she'd first met Rick Dicker and he'd offered her a position with the NSA in his calm, straightforward manner. Since then, she'd grown up, but he had stayed much the same. Even in his younger days he'd looked like a somewhat rumpled middle-aged man. The style of his suits and ties hadn't changed. In fact, he might have been wearing the very suit he had on today when he'd spoken at her high school assembly.

Dicker replaced his glasses and seemed to be studying her.

"Are you going to make me guess?" Elastigirl said, bringing her feet back to the floor and straightening the chair.

"You have proved to be one of our very

best. You complete your assignments with little damage. You have the goodwill of the public. You take initiative without being reckless."

Elastigirl raised an eyebrow. "Please," she said drily. "You're going to make me blush." She leaned forward and placed her elbows on Dicker's desk, resting her chin in her hands. "What's up?"

"We would like to offer you a team."

Surprised, Elastigirl sat back in the chair as Dicker flipped open a file folder on his desk. "You would lead two others who are already paired," he said, consulting the papers. "It would come with a pay raise—"

Elastigirl held up her hand to stop him from going any further. "Hang on. You want me to be a team leader? I don't think so."

"You really should hear me out," Dicker said.

"I don't need to."

"We at the NSA all see great team-leader qualities in you."

"Except the most important one," Elastigirl argued. "See, I don't *want* to be a team leader. I don't even want to be on a team. You know that."

"I think you'd find the challenge exciting," Dicker said.

"Challenge?" Elastigirl repeated. She crossed her arms. "I see. You've got a problem on your hands and you think I'm the one who can solve it?"

A ghost of a smile flickered on Dicker's lips. "As I said. You know me too well."

"Okay, now I'm curious," Elastigirl said. "But only because I'm nosy, not because I'm actually interested in taking the position."

"We'll see," Dicker said. "This is the situation." He flipped the file shut. "We have a Super who the NSA has determined works best partnered. But she can be difficult." He gave Elastigirl a look over the rims of his glasses. "Like you," he continued, "she is gutsy and strong-willed."

"A Super has to be," Elastigirl protested.

"Agreed. To a point, that is. She has already burned through one partnership—" Dicker paused and gave a little laugh. "Oh, that's good. *Burned.*" Elastigirl's puzzled look must have tipped him off that she didn't get the joke. "Because of her powers," he added.

"Uh-huh . . ." She twirled a finger, indicating he should get to the point.

Dicker cleared his throat and consulted his file again. "In any case, she is now on a new team, and already there are issues. We feel that a trio, rather than a duo, would smooth things out."

"Less butting heads, someone to act as mediator and tiebreaker," Elastigirl said, nodding.

"Exactly."

Elastigirl stood. "You're right—that would be a challenge. And a major headache. I'm not interested in being the babysitter and peacemaker for squabbling Supers."

Dicker sighed. "I told them you wouldn't want it. But I promised I would try."

Elastigirl smiled. "I'm glad to know that we understand each other." She sat back down. "I was worried for a minute there, Rick. If you were behind this so-called promotion, I would have to assume you didn't know me as well as I thought you did."

Dicker smiled back. "I do think you'd be good for it. I think you might be one of the few Supers Blazestone would listen to."

"Blazestone?" Elastigirl said. "Hoo-boy. Now I'm really glad I turned you down."

Despite being a relatively new member of the NSA, Blazestone was already becoming something of a legend. Her powers included pyrotechnic blasts, giving the impression she was a fireworks-producing machine. Only her fireworks weren't exactly celebratory; they could be lethal. She could fly by riding on currents of heated air, a skill Elastigirl had to admit she envied. For a while, Blazestone had been partnered with Frozone; the NSA had probably thought Blazestone's heat met with Frozone's cool would be a good balance. But it hadn't worked out. Frozone was a pretty laid-back guy, but Elastigirl knew Blazestone had managed to drive him up a wall. She was argumentative, only wanted to do things her way, and never turned up on time for anything. In spite of all that, Frozone still admired Blazestone's skills, her spunk, and her willingness to throw herself into the fray 1,000 percent. More than once he had told Elastigirl that she and Blazestone had some similar qualities.

"Who do you have her working with now?" Elastigirl asked.

"Universal Man."

Elastigirl laughed. "Wow, I *really* dodged a bullet, didn't I? Universal Man agreed to having a leader? I can't imagine it." It was hard for her to picture Universal Man taking orders from anyone other than an official from the NSA. Even then he sometimes complained.

"Well . . . we didn't exactly tell him yet," Dicker admitted. "We were waiting to hear what you had to say."

"And now you've heard me."

Dicker sighed. "Loud and clear."

CHAPTER 3

A few hours later, Elastigirl stood staring into the face of a familiar enemy: her mostly empty refrigerator. A sad, limp carrot. Strawberry yogurt past its expiration date. One slice of American cheese.

Elastigirl sighed. After a morning full of stretchy crime-stopping, not to mention her meeting with Dicker, she was positively starving. "Well, this won't do," she said as she shut the fridge door. "Time for a grocery run."

She strolled into her bedroom and rummaged through her dresser. "Jeans, check. Sweatshirt, check. Cowboy boots, check left and check right." She slipped everything on over her Supersuit, then faced the full-length mirror hanging on the back of her bedroom door.

"Hello, Helen Highwater," she said. "Check." She grinned at her reflection. Then she cocked her head, studying herself. Something was off. . . .

"Ooops!" she said with a giggle. She pulled off her mask and slid it into the back pocket of her jeans. Looking into the mirror again, she fiddled with the crime alert button on her headband until it was how she wanted it. She was ready.

She grabbed the oversized purse that sat beside the front door. In it went her spiffy (not to mention *stretchy*) Elastigirl boots and her other Super accessories. After all, she always had to be prepared for anything and everything.

Then she left to greet the world as Helen Highwater, Elastigirl's secret identity. Most Supers had them, and Elastigirl found hers immensely helpful. After all, it would be pretty hard to go about your day doing chores and running errands as a Super. People would stop you for an autograph, or to take a picture, or to ask you to do things for them that didn't truly qualify for a Super's intervention.

Just the week before when she had been out patrolling, a man in matching sweats had come running down the stoop of his brownstone, calling for Elastigirl's help. Elastigirl had rushed to his aid. She'd followed the fellow up the steps and into his apartment on the top floor.

"Where's the perp?" Elastigirl had asked as the man hurried into the kitchen. He charged back out, holding a jar of sliced peaches.

"It's a crime how hard it is to open these things," the man had complained. "And I can't eat my oatmeal without my peaches."

Elastigirl had blinked at him a few times. "Seriously? This is why you called for me?"

"Don't you think they should be easier to open?" the man demanded. "Of course, I'm sure it's never a problem for you. But what about the rest of us?"

Elastigirl had sighed and twisted the jar lid.

She never minded helping out, but that situation hadn't exactly required her special abilities. What if there had been a real emergency elsewhere that needed her attention—like a cat in a tall tree, a jailbreak, or worse, a Super Villain out on a mission of destruction and mayhem? Today, she just wanted to grab a few things from the store with no detours.

It was a beautiful day, so she strolled to the grocery store, enjoying the sights and sounds of her beloved city. She was even enjoying her anonymity, for once able to simply observe rather than be observed herself. Leave the limelight to the Supers who wanted it; that was her attitude.

A little while later, Helen was pushing her shopping cart down the cereal aisle. "Now, if I were a jumbo-sized box of Super Crunch Crunchies, where would I be . . . ?" she murmured. She spotted the colorful box on the top shelf. "Ah! There you are."

She stood on tiptoe and strained to reach it. But her fingers couldn't quite grasp it. She flattened her feet again and let out a puff of air in frustration.

Then she raised an eyebrow. *Should I . . . ?* She glanced around. The coast was clear. Her hand was *s-t-r-e-t-c-h-i-n-g* toward the giant box of cereal when a large man barreled around the corner of the aisle with an overloaded shopping cart. Helen froze mid-reach and snapped her hand back into place.

Luckily, the man was studying his three-page shopping list as he zoomed along the aisle. He glanced up and scanned the shelves, his gaze coming to rest on Helen. He skidded to a stop. "Need some help there?" he asked.

"What?" Helen stared at him a moment before realizing she was still on her toes, and her arm, though normal length, was still above her head. She covered by running her hand through her hair and resuming a regular standing position. "Naw. I'm good."

"Well, if you're sure," the man said, his blue eyes twinkling.

Helen glanced at his shopping cart brimming with groceries. "Looks like you're stocking up for hibernation," she said. "Or shopping for a party."

"Just my regular list," he replied with a grin. "A big guy requires big fuel."

"Makes sense." Helen smiled up at him. He *was* a big guy; he towered over her.

He studied his list again, flipping pages and checking things in his cart. While his eyes were averted, Helen quickly stretched up her hand, snatched the cereal, and tossed it into her cart.

"Looks like I'm done here," the man said. "How about you?"

"Yup. Shopping, check."

"Excuse me?" The guy looked confused.

Helen felt a flush creep along her cheeks. "Oh, that's just something I do to make sure I'm not forgetting anything. You know, 'Keys, check. Wallet, check–' "

"Checkbook, check," the guy said.

"Exactly," Helen said.

The big man looked down to meet her eyes. "I do the same thing," he confessed.

They laughed and started down the aisle. Helen and the blond stranger chatted all the way to checkout. She was surprised how easy it was to shoot the breeze with a non-Super.

When Helen finished paying, she carried her shopping bags to where the man was standing at the door, studying a poster. He held multiple shopping bags against his broad chest.

Helen was curious why the poster held his interest. " 'Supers Appreciation Day,' " she read.

"They sure have a lot of neat activities planned for that," the guy said. "Kids' games, a costume contest, and then the awards ceremony."

"What awards ceremony?" Helen asked. She already knew about the event; all the Supers did. The NSA had convinced the mayor of Municiberg to create a citywide holiday to honor the Supers. It seemed kind of silly. People taking pictures with Supers, fans dressing up like Supers. But she hadn't heard about any awards ceremony. "What are the awards for?"

The man peered more closely at the poster. "Wow. Looks like the Super who has caught the most criminals in the last year is given a medal and a key to the city. There are all kinds of other awards, too. Fan Favorite. Most Improved . . ."

"Hmm. They must have just added those," Helen said.

"That ought to be pretty motivating for the Supers," the man said, shifting his overstuffed shopping bags.

"I think we're—I mean, *they're*—already pretty motivated," Helen countered. "Part of being a Super, right? It's their duty to help protect the city. I don't understand why there needs to be a whole day set aside just to have people fawn over them."

"I suppose. . . . Still, it looks like a fine way to spend an afternoon. For Supers and regular folks."

Helen frowned. "I don't know. A Super's job is to fight crime, not spend time posing for pictures."

The guy balanced his shopping bags so he could scratch his head. "Maybe. But look at it this way: everyone needs a little appreciation when they've been working hard. Supers are no different. Why, I myself . . ." He stopped himself with a cough. "Why, I believe that without the goodwill of the public, the Supers could have a harder time fighting crime."

"Hmmm . . ." Helen thought back to earlier that morning. She might not have been able to catch Mysterious Melvin if that motorcyclist hadn't been willing to hand off his bike to her, no questions asked. And it had been because of how much that motorcyclist admired Supers. Maybe this guy had a point. "I guess I see what you're saying," Helen said. Still, she wasn't sure Supers needed an entire *day* of appreciation.

They stepped out of the store into the warm afternoon. As they did, a little girl holding the hand of an elderly lady slowly approached. The brawny man leaned against the door, keeping it open for them while he balanced his many overloaded bags.

The little girl tugged on the white-haired lady's hand. "C'mon, Grandma. He's waiting for us."

"Don't rush me," the woman snapped.

"No need to hurry, my friend," the man said with a grin. "Take all the time you need."

"Now that's how a polite person behaves," the woman scolded the child.

Eventually, the pair made it to the door. The white-haired woman stopped and patted the guy's hand. A hand that was trying to maintain its grip on the shopping bags.

"Thank you so much," she said in a creaky voice. "Young people these days always seem to be in such a hurry."

Helen could see the man's grocery bags starting to wobble a little in their precarious position. But he just said, "One misses so much by dashing about."

"So true. But I'm not always in the slow lane," the woman said.

"No?" the man asked, shifting a bit to keep hold of the door and his bags.

"Oh, no. You should see me in my speed-walking class. I can walk circles around the others. But I pick and choose when and where I pick up my pace. You look like you must exercise, too."

"Grandma . . ." the little girl began.

"The nice man and I are talking," Grandma told the girl.

Helen wondered how long it would be before the man's grocery bags went tumbling to the ground. She freed one of her arms in case she needed to reach out to grab one.

Grandma pulled a lint-covered mint from a pocket in her yellow cardigan. "Have a candy."

"I . . . uh . . ." The man looked at his full hands and shot Helen a *help me* look.

"Here, I'll hold it for him." Helen stepped forward to accept the fuzzy mint.

"Well . . ." Grandma eyed Helen suspiciously. "If you're sure . . ." Her hand hovered above Helen's as she squinted up at the man, uncertain.

"Oh, you can trust her," the man assured her.

"All right, then," Grandma relented. She dropped the mint into Helen's hand. "Lovely chatting with you." She and her granddaughter walked into the store.

The big man instantly shifted around the heavy bags as he released the door. "Whoo. That's better," he said.

"That was very nice of you," Helen told him. She held up the mint and raised her eyebrow.

The man shook his head, then shrugged. "It's nice to be nice."

He and Helen started walking again. Helen tossed the lint-covered mint into the trash can on the corner. She noticed the streets were a little more crowded. People were getting out of work.

"So maybe you'll go to the Supers Appreciation Day parade?" the man said. "I've heard there are some good costumes."

Helen smirked. If he only knew . . . Dressing as *Helen* could be considered a costume! "I don't think so."

"Oh, well . . . I thought I'd see you there." He

let out a chuckle as he shook his head. "Whoops, I never even introduced myself! I'm Bob Parr." He wiggled his fingers, which were still wrapped around his shopping bags. "I'd shake, but . . ."

"Helen," Elastigirl said. She shifted her own grocery bag so she could take one of his fingers. She shook it. "Nice to meet you."

"Back atcha."

They looked at each other for a moment. Elastigirl had the feeling he was about to ask her to attend the Supers Appreciation Day festivities with him. But before they could get into an awkward conversation, she spun on her heel. "Okay then. I'd better scram. Bye now!" she called over her shoulder.

She was surprised by how disappointed she was to think she'd never see him again. *There's no future with a non-Super,* she told herself.

Besides, she was a go-solo kind of gal.

CHAPTER 4

Why did he seem so familiar? Helen mulled over her conversation with Bob Parr as she walked home. She couldn't escape the nagging feeling that she'd met him before. But that wasn't possible, was it? It wasn't like she knew a lot of non-Supers. Most of her days were spent Super-ing or training; any free time she had was for recouping and sometimes hanging out with her Super friends. Or trying to fit in errands.

Helen peeked into her grocery bag while she waited for the traffic light to change. What to make for her meal? *A simple plate of scrambled eggs,* she decided.

The light turned green. She had just stepped

off the curb when she heard a scream. Then a shout. And a shriek!

People streamed around the corner as if they were racing for their lives.

"What's going on?" Helen shouted.

No one answered. They were too busy running away.

She couldn't use her power to stretch above the crowd, not dressed as Helen and in front of all these people. Frustrated, she set down her shopping bag and clambered up onto the square base of a nearby streetlamp. *Regular folks do this all the time, don't they?* Helen thought as she gripped the pole and leaned out, taking care not to stretch too far.

A tiger padded down the street, sending cars careening out of the way, tires screeching.

Sheesh. More traffic problems. Then Helen did a double take.

Wait. *What?*

Her mouth dropped open. *A tiger?* A tiger in downtown Municiberg?

The powerful creature let out a yowl and leapt onto the hood of a parked car, snarling.

The zoo, she remembered. It wasn't too far away. The animal must have escaped. She had wanted to see the zoo's newest resident, but certainly not like this!

The tiger jumped off the car and bounded down the now-deserted street.

Time to get into action! Helen looked both ways. The crowd seemed to have cleared out. She had just started to get into Super mode when she heard shouts above her. Whoops! People were hanging out of their open windows, craning their necks and trying to watch where the tiger went.

Where could she don her mask and drop her outer clothes without being seen? Helen scanned the area. The office buildings wouldn't have any rooms she could use. Going back to the grocery store wouldn't do anything but waste time. And she couldn't exactly knock on apartment doors in the buildings on the other side of the street, going in as Helen and coming out as Elastigirl. Plus, the news copter that had appeared overhead meant she couldn't just duck down behind a car. Her transformation would be caught on camera.

Then she spotted it: a porta-potty at the

construction site across the street. Helen sighed. It wasn't exactly ideal, but she didn't have time to find a better place. She jumped down off the base of the streetlamp.

Leaving her groceries behind, she dashed to the construction site. First a garbage truck, now this. *I wonder,* she thought as she shut and locked the porta-potty door behind her, *is tomorrow going to be as smelly as today?*

A few seconds later, Elastigirl quickly stepped out of the porta-potty in full Super mode. She immediately let out the breath she'd been holding with a *whoosh*, tugging the top of her left boot. She had switched shoes in such a hurry to get out of that smelly box she was surprised she'd actually gotten the boots on the right feet.

Not wanting to waste any more time, Elastigirl raced to the corner. "Okay, tiger. Where are you?"

She didn't see the animal, but it soon became easy to figure out which way it had gone. She just had to head in the direction everyone else was running *from*.

Sure enough, Elastigirl soon found a panicked

crowd surging from a side street. *All right, the tiger must be down there,* Elastigirl reasoned.

"Coming through! Super here! Outta the way, please!" she called as she darted among the terrified citizens. She burst through the mass of people onto an empty tree-lined side street.

Well, it was almost empty.

Mr. Incredible stood in the middle of the road, knees bent, arms wide. He was staring down the tiger, which was pacing back and forth, growling and flicking its tail.

Elastigirl put on a burst of speed and used her super-stretched legs to close the distance.

"Here, kitty, kitty!" she called to get the tiger's attention.

The tiger swung its head around and fixed its gaze on her.

"The crime alert didn't go off," Elastigirl called to Mr. Incredible. "What are you doing here?"

"I was in the neighborhood," he shouted back. "What are *you* doing here?"

"I guess I have a knack for being in the right place at the right time!"

Elastigirl focused on the animal in front of her. The tiger's whiskers twitched as it considered her, catching her scent. Its powerful muscles rippled under its striped fur with each step. Elastigirl could see the fear in its eyes and knew it was even more dangerous because it felt cornered—parked cars all around, one Super in front of it, and one Super behind. The tiger snarled at her, revealing large, sharp, lethal teeth.

Elastigirl gulped.

"Over here!" Mr. Incredible shouted at the big cat. "She's so rubbery she wouldn't even make a decent snack! Hard to chew!"

Elastigirl rolled her eyes as the tiger turned back to its original prey. Mr. Incredible fixed his masked gaze on the animal and the tiger stared right back at him.

It lowered its body as if preparing to pounce. It licked its lips.

Elastigirl glanced around the area to formulate a plan. Noticing a perfectly positioned tree, she darted behind the tiger while its full attention was still on Mr. Incredible. She stretched her arms and swung herself up into the sprawling oak that stood right behind the tiger, the tree's branches reaching out into the street. The animal seemed frozen. Was it too afraid to make a move, or was it gathering its strength?

Mr. Incredible glanced up to where Elastigirl shimmied along a thick branch. "Are you trying to get that award?"

"What award?" she asked. *Just a few more inches and I should be in position.*

"For most criminals apprehended! The one they're giving out on Supers Appreciation Day."

"I don't think that a tiger qualifies as a criminal!" *Sheesh!* Elastigirl shook her head. "Besides, the award isn't as pressing as Mr. Claws down there. Can we please deal with the problem at hand?"

"Don't worry about it. I'll get it in a jiffy!" Mr. Incredible shouted—just as the tiger pounced with a loud roar. It knocked Mr. Incredible onto his back and leapt on top of him.

"No, I don't think you will!" Elastigirl lowered herself down along the branch. Thinking quickly, she *r-e-a-c-h-e-d* down from her perch high above the street and grasped the tiger by the scruff of its neck. It was just like grabbing a kitten—a humongous, heavy kitten with extremely sharp teeth.

The tiger yowled, turning and snapping those enormous teeth, trying to bite Elastigirl's hands to get her to let go. But it couldn't reach her without moving off Mr. Incredible, and it seemed determined to keep the Super trapped beneath it.

Elastigirl strengthened her grip. She managed to lift the tiger high enough for Mr. Incredible to roll out from underneath the struggling big cat. The tiger let out a furious roar, kicking its legs, squirming, and frantically trying to break free.

"Hey! I was handling it!" Mr. Incredible protested as he scrambled to his feet.

"It looked more like the tiger was handling *you*!" Elastigirl retorted.

She peered down at the tiger. It was heftier than she had expected, and its terror made its movements frenetic and jerky. "Okay," she murmured, gritting her teeth a bit from the effort to keep hold of the tiger as it fought to escape. "Now that I've got you, big kitty, what am I going to do with you?"

She had to get the animal back to its home at

the zoo, safely and without anyone getting hurt in the process. So she'd have to stay far above the ground . . . even if the tiger wasn't so crazy about being airborne.

Elastigirl wrapped her elastic arms several times around the tiger and tied her wrists in a knot for good measure. She didn't want to lose her grip on this baby. Then she slowly stretched a leg until it landed on a branch of the neighboring tree. Her body widened and flattened as she crept from tree to tree, the tiger dangling high above the street.

She carefully made it to the corner. Shocked cries and screams filled the air as people on Main Street spotted Elastigirl and the tiger above them. A crowd quickly formed, pointing and shouting. This terrified the poor tiger even more, and again it roared and struggled to get free, trying to reach Elastigirl's hands with its teeth and taking swipes at her wrapped arms with its huge paws. She managed to avoid the deadly claws by reshaping her limbs, moving them out of the way of the tiger's attacks, without losing the hold she had around its heavy body.

Mr. Incredible followed below. "Don't worry! I'll back you up!"

"No need!" she called down to him. She snorted. Why would he think she'd need his help?

Only, there was one problem. She had been concentrating so hard on keeping her grip on the tiger that she'd lost track of the street signs. She rarely got lost, but she was moving by feel alone—focusing on what tree was nearest—so that she could keep the tiger high above the people below. Somewhere along the way, the trees had led her in a crooked pattern. "Which way to the zoo?" she shouted above the tiger's roar.

Mr. Incredible raised an eyebrow and put his hands on his hips. A smirk appeared on his face, making Elastigirl regret the question. Luckily, before Mr. Incredible could make a smart remark, someone in the crowd shouted, "It's three blocks that way!" and five people pointed to Elastigirl's left.

"Thanks!" Elastigirl continued her slow progress, moving from tree to tree and leaving Mr. Incredible behind her. She was starting to sweat and really glad she'd thought to tie her hands.

Otherwise, she might have lost her grip on the tiger. Elastigirl was stretched to the max in all directions, but she couldn't hurry. She didn't want to risk slamming the poor yowling tiger into anything—or anyone. Some of the crowd was following along down below. She really wished they wouldn't do that; it continued to put them in danger, and it frightened the tiger. But she didn't want to scare the tiger even more by shouting down at them to clear the area.

"We gotta be getting close. . . ." Elastigirl's breath was starting to get ragged. She wasn't sure how much longer she could keep this up. Then she spotted the zoo gates. "Yes!" she huffed. Now that they were almost there, Elastigirl felt renewed energy.

But she'd just run out of trees.

"Okay, kitty, it's going to get a little bumpy now," Elastigirl told the tiger.

She took a deep breath. "And . . . now!" She hurled herself off the tree and onto the top of the zoo's entrance gate. The tiger let out a howl as Elastigirl twisted, swinging the tiger up and over the gate. Its weight and momentum yanked

Elastigirl off her precarious perch, and they tumbled head over tail into the zoo.

Before they slammed into the ground, Elastigirl shot out her feet and arms. She stretched her fingers, still crisscrossed and tied behind the tiger's back, to clutch the weather vane on top of the zoo's gift shop near the entrance. She wobbled but stayed upright. The tiger roared and clawed at the air but was unhurt.

"Just a few more minutes," Elastigirl told the tiger. "You're almost home." She steadied herself and released the weather vane. She stood just inside the front entrance with every limb stretched. She had to twist her head through some tree branches to peer down into the zoo. A uniformed zookeeper raced toward her.

"Uh . . . where does this furry fellow belong?" she asked him.

"This way!" the zookeeper replied. "I'll show you."

Staying tall, Elastigirl carefully held the tiger with stretched arms a safe distance from her super-stretched body. It continued to wriggle and roar.

She felt bad for the frightened animal. *She* knew this was for its own good, but *it* certainly didn't. "I know, kitty, it's all very scary. But it will be over very soon and you'll be back home, safe and sound."

She followed the zookeeper to the tiger's habitat and gently lowered it inside. Unfurling her arms, she sent the tiger rolling along the grassy turf. Set free, the big cat bounded up onto a large boulder, turned its back on Elastigirl, and immediately began grooming itself. A moment later it let out a loud purr and settled down for a nap.

Elastigirl zipped all her limbs back to their proper lengths, widths, and positions. She brushed her hair off her face and fixed her headband. *Phew.* She was glad that was over! No one got hurt, and the tiger seemed very happy to be back home. She wondered if Mr. Incredible had followed along with the crowd. She snorted. Nah. He probably went off to practice his acceptance speech for all those awards he thought he was going to win.

"Thank you, thank you, thank you!" The zookeeper gripped Elastigirl's hand in both of his and pumped her arm up and down furiously. "Thank you!"

"All in a Super-day's work," she told him.

He continued shaking her hand. "Well, you have my vote for the Super-est Super on Appreciation Day."

"Vote?" Elastigirl repeated, gingerly removing her hand from his.

"Oh, yes! The Fan Favorite award! At first I was going to vote for Mr. Incredible, but after today? It's definitely you."

"Well, thank you for that," Elastigirl said, warmed by his kind and enthusiastic words despite herself. "Now, you just make sure kitty over there isn't too upset by his adventure today. And be sure to keep all the gates locked."

The zookeeper nodded several times. "Of course. We'll be double- and triple-checking from now on!" he assured her.

"I'm sure you will."

As Elastigirl strolled through the entrance gates, she heard him calling after her. "Quadruple-checking! Quint—uh, quinto—uh, we'll even check five times! Just to be sure!"

Elastigirl shook her head with a smile.

But the smile faded when she realized her groceries were all the way back on the other side of town. And her Helen outfit lay crumpled on the floor of a porta-potty.

She headed back and found her food bags had been trampled by the panicked bystanders. Elastigirl sighed, tossing the muddy remains into a trash can. "Looks like it's going to be a takeout kind of night," she said to no one in particular. Then she began to trudge back to the porta-potty to retrieve her pocketbook and street clothes. There was no way she was going to abandon her favorite cowboy boots.

CHAPTER 5

Elastigirl unlocked her apartment door, looking forward to washing off the day. The walk back to the porta-potty had felt endless. And it had added at least an extra mile to what was supposed to have been a simple trip to the grocery store. Well, some days were just like that as a Super.

As she crossed her threshold, she kicked an envelope that had been slipped under the door while she was out. When she picked it up, she saw the NSA logo stamped on the front. "What's this about?" she wondered as she ripped open the envelope. She pulled out several pages of official-looking forms.

Flipping through the papers, she reached her other arm through the swinging door to the kitchen. Her hand riffled through her collection of well-used takeout menus. She knew by size, shape, and degree of wear and tear which menu was which without even looking.

"'Voluntary test subjects'?" she read, raising her eyebrows. "'NSA is seeking volunteers for experiments testing the viability of using a new compound, Zero Atomic Protocol, to enhance Super powers.' Hmmm . . ."

She brought the deli menu from the kitchen and placed it on her table, her eyes never leaving the NSA pages. She scanned the rest of the papers in the packet. "An application to become a volunteer. A liability waiver." She shook her head. "They want to test this stuff? On us?"

She stuffed the papers back in the envelope and tossed it aside. She didn't like the sound of Zero Atomic Protocol, not one bit. Besides, there were more pressing matters at hand. Perusing the deli menu, she decided on a roast beef on rye submarine sandwich and a bag of potato chips, grateful the restaurant delivered.

o o o

Mmmmmmm. Elastigirl shut her eyes and sank deeper into the bathtub. Lavender-scented bubbles tickled her nose.

She felt a thousand times better already. Her sandwich had been very satisfying. No more stinky smells from the garbage truck, the porta-potty, or the zoo. And her annoyance at that arrogant Mr. Incredible was completely washed away.

She dunked her head under the bubbles, then sat up, water streaming down her back. *It's not that he's a bad guy,* she mused. *After all, any friend of Frozone's must be* somewhat *cool.* She just wished he didn't have such a big ego. He could learn from that nice guy from the grocery store, Bob Parr. Now there was a guy who cared about helping people. Even chatty old ladies.

Elastigirl sighed, refocusing her attention on the Super-ing she had done that day. She always did her best thinking in a nice hot bath. And Rick Dicker had given her a lot to think about. She took pride in the idea that the NSA thought so highly of her that they would offer her such a challenging team-leadership position. But that didn't mean she wanted to accept it. Still, was it something to consider? Not Beta Force, Blazestone and Universal Man's team, but another one someday?

And then there was this new thing. "Zero Atomic Protocol," she said to herself. It didn't exactly roll off the tongue or sound very appealing. She wondered how the other Supers felt about it. Were any going to volunteer to experiment with it? Be guinea pigs?

She lathered up her hair with shampoo, wondering who would be the most likely to try it out.

Ding-dong!

Drat! Who could be at the door?

She stretched her neck so the rest of her could stay soaking in the tub. Her head traveled from the bathroom, around the corner, past her bedroom, and through the living room to the front door. She peeked out the peephole.

A tubby man in an ill-fitting suit stood beside a briefcase. In one arm he held an encyclopedia.

Ha! Glad I didn't get out of the bath for a door-to-door salesman.

The man pushed the doorbell again.

"No one home!" Elastigirl called through the door.

She retracted her neck. *Oops.* She had forgotten about the shampoo in her hair. A little trail of bubbles lay along the path her head had taken. *No problem,* she decided. *Just soap.*

She ran the hot water to bring the temperature in the tub back up. Okay, back to serious bathtub mulling.

Should she consider trying out that Zero stuff? Could it really help enhance her powers and make her Super-ing more efficient? She'd need to learn a whole lot more about it; that was for sure. She should make a list of everything she felt she needed to know.

"One," she said, trailing her hand through the bubbles.

Suddenly, the sound of a screechy violin came through her wall. Oh, dear. Her neighbor's little son Gerald must be having his music lesson.

"One," she repeated.

Screech, screech. Screech screech screech.

Elastigirl winced. The worst version of "Twinkle, Twinkle, Little Star" she'd ever heard intruded on her thinking. Okay. She had been making a list. But of what?

She had to drown out that awful sound. Her favorite radio show wouldn't start for a little while, but maybe some music would help.

Elastigirl stretched her arm out of the bathroom and down the hall. She connected with the radio in the living room and flicked it on. Swing music filled the apartment. It was a little too lively for her bathtub thinking time, so she switched to a different station. A singer with a velvety voice crooned a ballad. *Now that's the ticket!* She could barely hear Gerald's violin.

She brought back her hand and rinsed her hair, singing along with the radio. *Now what was I thinking about? Oh, right. That Zero Atomic Protocol stuff.* Nope. She wasn't going to try it out. At least, not yet.

What else . . . ? Taking over a team. She flicked bubbles into the air. *Nah,* she decided. The team thing just wasn't her.

Next she turned her mind to the upcoming Supers Appreciation Day. She hadn't volunteered for anything, since all that hoopla didn't interest her. But now . . .

Maybe that Bob Parr guy was onto something, she mused. She still wasn't so keen on a citywide Supers Appreciation Day, but it was nice to be thanked sometimes. Elastigirl often felt a little awkward when people expressed their gratitude, though she saw how important it had been to the zookeeper to say thank you. And she had to admit, the cheering of those motorcyclists when she'd gone after Mysterious Melvin had definitely given her a kick. Besides, it was the pride the citizens of Municiberg took in their Supers that had even made it possible for her to borrow Adam's motorcycle.

She scooped up a handful of bubbles and, with a puff of air, blew them around the bathroom. *What did that zookeeper say?* There was a "fan favorite" award. And Bob Parr had mentioned an award for the most criminals apprehended. She grinned as a bubble landed on her nose.

She was no fan of egomaniacs, but maybe it wouldn't be so bad to be recognized for what she did . . . in a tasteful way, of course. And she'd enjoy the challenge of working toward earning the award for most criminals caught.

She burst the soap bubble on her nose and laughed. She'd love to see the look on Mr. Incredible's face if she won the award instead of him.

But no, Elastigirl decided, *I'm not in this for the glory.* Awards were fine and dandy, and maybe they motivated the other Supers, but they weren't what motivated her. Her primary concern was doing all she could to keep Municiberg safe.

The phone rang. Well, it was time to get out anyway. Her fingers were like prunes. She reached her arm out to the living room again and picked up the phone. Since the cord wouldn't stretch very far, she stepped out of the tub, wrapped herself in a towel, and headed over to the receiver.

"Hello?" she said into the phone. Reaching her other arm all the way back to the bathroom, she grabbed another towel and wrapped her hair in it.

"Hey, Elastigirl! It's Apogee."

"Hi, Gee," Elastigirl said.

Another Super, Apogee had powers that were generated with solar energy. She wore a special suit that could reflect sunbeams, which Apogee used to start fires if needed. Her suit could also absorb the sun's power for her to convert into superhot blasts. Elastigirl had enjoyed spending time with Apogee ever since the high-spirited Super had moved to Municiberg from Arizona.

"What's up?" Elastigirl asked. She returned the towel to the rack with her toes and stood on two feet again.

"Blazestone and I are going to see a movie," Apogee said. "Wanna join?"

"I didn't know you and Blazestone were friends," Elastigirl said.

"Yeah, sure. We got to know each other doing the Blast-a-thons. You know, the events where the Supers who generate energy blasts compete on accuracy, distance, and firepower?"

"Oh, right," Elastigirl said. "I wish I'd managed to get to those. Somehow I was always sent on reconnaissance by the NSA or otherwise engaged."

"You would have loved them," Apogee said.

"And Blazestone, she was the only Super who gave me serious competition. She has mad skills."

That didn't surprise Elastigirl. If Blazestone had been recruited by the NSA, she must have something special to offer. And it made sense she would get along with Apogee; they had a lot in common with their similar blasting powers.

"So, whaddya say?"

"Sure." Elastigirl was already reaching for the clothes in her bedroom with a stretched arm while she grabbed the hair dryer from under the bathroom sink. It might be nice to get out of the house to do something fun. Besides, Elastigirl was curious about Blazestone and intrigued by the idea of getting to know her better. "Are we meeting as our secret identities?"

"Blazestone said she's more comfortable as her Super self."

Most Supers relied on their secret identities to move about the world inconspicuously. Some Supers had even found ways to incorporate their skills when in secret-identity mode. The Phylange, one of the other members of Apogee's former team, the Thrilling Three, was one such Super.

His power was sonic voice projection. So it made sense that he was an opera singer in his non-Super life.

On the other hand, some Supers rarely went out into the world without their masks and Supersuits. Universal Man, for example, refused to use a secret identity. He was *always* in Super mode: always masked, always wearing his suit. Elastigirl wondered if maybe Blazestone's reluctance to appear in public as anything other than her Super self was because her partner, Universal Man, never did.

"Supers it is," Elastigirl said. "Be there in ten minutes."

ooo

Elastigirl spotted Blazestone and Apogee in front of the duplex movie theater. Pedestrians gawked as they strolled by. She wondered if appearing in their Supersuits hadn't been such a great idea. Still, no one seemed to be pestering Blazestone and Apogee, and she saw only admiration in those who noticed them. Every now and then someone would come over to say hi or thank them for their service. She supposed at least they'd be prepared should any crime stopping be needed.

"Sorry I took so long," Elastigirl said when she joined them under the marquee. A light rain was falling. She gazed down at her feet. "I have to rely on these to get me where I'm going."

Apogee slung her arm over Elastigirl's shoulder. "At least your powers work after dark." The solar-powered Super glanced up at the darkening sky.

"Yeah," Blazestone said, twisting the end of her ponytail. "And your stretchy powers don't go on the fritz in the rain. Even this dumb drizzle could interfere with mine."

"Rain does me in, too," Apogee said. "And I'm pretty useless after sunset if my suit isn't already charged up. You're lucky your powers aren't weather-dependent."

"I suppose..." Elastigirl conceded. "Still, I could use some more transportation options."

"Maybe the NSA can hook you up," Blazestone suggested.

"Hey, have you heard about this new thing the NSA is testing?" Apogee asked. "ZAP?"

"ZAP?" Elastigirl asked.

"Zero Atomic Protocol," Apogee replied.

"Oh, yeah. I got that packet of info this afternoon." Elastigirl shuddered. "Sounds strange. Why would they be experimenting with it?"

"It's a way to recycle," Apogee explained enthusiastically. "We produce an awful lot of leftover atomic energy. The NSA wants to figure out something to do with it all. We really do need to be mindful of our waste products."

Elastigirl remembered how involved Apogee was in different environmental causes. Her secret identity was a spokesperson for the benefits of solar energy.

"What's this ZAP stuff for?" Blazestone asked. "I didn't bother wading through all that paper."

"Well, they're still working on it," Apogee explained. "They were wondering if they could use it as a kind of protective covering—coating doors leading to supersensitive offices or painting it onto fences and bank safes. It would limit access to only those who have been given special gloves and are trained in how to handle it. Which would *not* be the bad guys."

"Hmmm." Elastigirl thought that was a pretty complicated way to keep things protected.

"But they also think it might enhance a Super's powers!" Apogee said. "They're asking for volunteers and I already signed up. I'm starting testing tomorrow."

Blazestone raised an eyebrow and glanced at Elastigirl.

"I don't know, Apogee," Elastigirl said. "It sounds kinda dangerous to me."

"I don't want the NSA monkeying around with me and my powers," Blazestone said in agreement.

"I'm surprised they would experiment on Supers with something so unknown," Elastigirl said. "Is it dangerous?"

Apogee shrugged. "We'll take precautions."

"There's probably a whole load of paperwork that goes along with it," Blazestone said. "The NSA is all bureaucracy and red tape!" She shook her head. Then she gave them each a wink. "I'd say we're all pretty awesome just as we are."

"I'll second that," Elastigirl said.

Blazestone grinned at Elastigirl and held up a

hand for a fist bump. Smiling, Elastigirl tapped it with hers.

The rain started to come down harder.

"I see what you guys are saying," Apogee said. "But I'm curious to learn more. Especially if it helps with the limitations on my powers."

The line started to move slowly.

"Speaking of powers, get this," Blazestone said as the three started walking forward. "The other day, I was zooming through the air after a criminal and was throwing some nice fiery blasts, when what do I see? A gang of dognappers Universal Man and I had been trying to bring in for, like, a week."

"Criminals can be so inconsiderate," Apogee joked. "It's like they go out of their way to make our lives difficult!"

"Always turning up at the most inconvenient times!" Elastigirl said, smiling. "So who'd you go after?"

"Everybody!" Blazestone said. "A zip here, a zap there, and wham!" She clapped her hands loudly, startling the guy waiting in line in front of her. He glared at her over his shoulder. Apogee shot him a fierce look and he turned back around.

"A nice big bad-guy haul," Blazestone said. "If I do say so myself."

"You're a shoo-in for that Appreciation Day award," Apogee said. She knocked her shoulder into Blazestone's. "As long as it's not raining," she teased.

Blazestone laughed. "Think maybe the NSA can get started on trying to control the weather? I want to make a spectacular entrance when I pick up that trophy."

Elastigirl wanted to reserve judgment until she got to know Blazestone better, but she was starting to see why the partnership with Frozone hadn't worked out. He was so laid-back and humble, and Blazestone was one high-intensity and somewhat braggy Super. Elastigirl wondered how Universal Man was dealing with Blazestone's... *assertiveness* now that the NSA had them working together. But of course, there was nothing wrong with self-confidence, and Universal Man had quite the ego of his own.

"Did I ever tell you about the time I was sent on

a mission for the NSA into the desert?" Apogee asked. "This was back when I was still in Arizona. They knew I could handle the heat, the sun, what have you. None of us realized how much sun power my suit absorbed, and there was no shade. Not anywhere." She started giggling.

"What happened?" Elastigirl asked.

"Well, I gathered the intel and signaled I was coming back in. The bigwigs were all very excited by the success of the mission; we had found the desert hideout of a notorious gang. When I got back to headquarters, I really wanted to get out of the suit. I was covered in dust and had more than a few cactus needles poking into me, which made it impossible to sit down."

Elastigirl and Blazestone laughed.

"So I went into the locker room, where I had my secret identity clothes stashed," Apogee continued. "I got out of the suit and tossed it in the laundry bin. I was really looking forward to that shower. But then... *Whoopsie!* The smell of towels on fire got me out of that shower, pronto!" She shook her head, chortling. "Of course they went up in flames. What had I been thinking? With all that stored solar energy, I could have fried eggs on that suit!"

Laughing loudly, the three Supers reached the box office and bought their tickets. While they looked for seats in the crowded movie theater, Apogee continued telling stories of her training mishaps. "Oh, my," she said with a chuckle. "Then there was the time when I accidentally gave the head of the NSA field office a sunburn. I thought I was cooked for sure! It didn't help that it happened when he was demonstrating a new mask. When he took it off he had white patches where the mask had been, lost in a sea of lobster-red skin!"

"Stop!" Elastigirl laughed. "You're making my sides ache."

Blazestone guffawed. "Girlfriend, I am surprised you survived training. No! I'm surprised *anyone* survived your training. I have *never* heard so many ridiculous mistakes!" Then she smirked at Apogee. "Wait a sec. Did all of those crazy things *really* happen?"

Apogee smirked back. "I'm not telling."

"Even if they didn't," Elastigirl said, still laughing, "they make for excellent stories."

The three Supers settled into seats. "Oh! We forgot to get popcorn!" Blazestone craned her neck toward the exit, then faced the screen again. A movie trailer had just started.

"No problem! I can take care of it." Elastigirl pulled out a bill and then stretched her arms out to the lobby concessions stand. She held up three fingers of one hand. Luckily, this was a movie theater Supers often attended, so the snack bar attendant knew exactly what to do. Elastigirl felt the bill being taken and then three bags of popcorn were placed carefully into her hands. A moment later, she passed Apogee and Blazestone their bags of popcorn.

The movie title blazed across the screen. . . .

Just as the crime signal button on Elastigirl's headband started dinging.

"Crime in progress!" She jumped up. She looked at her friends.

"If that ZAP worked, I could go with you right now!" Apogee complained.

Blazestone frowned as she stood. "Do you think it stopped raining?"

"Only one way to find out," Elastigirl said as she and Blazestone rose.

"Excuse me, pardon me, excuse me," Elastigirl said to the people whose view of the screen she was blocking as she made her way down the aisle. "Pardon me, crime in progress, excuse me."

She scooted out of the theater and into the lobby, Blazestone right behind her. They stopped in front of the glass doors.

"Sorry, Blaze," Elastigirl said. "It's a downpour out there."

Blazestone gritted her teeth in frustration and stamped a booted foot, sending out a spark. Elastigirl sympathized. She could see how much it irked the Super to be unable to go into crime-fighting mode. Though Blazestone seemed to be a bit of a hothead, Elastigirl did admire the Super's passion for her work.

"Want me to call for any backup?" Blazestone asked with a sigh.

"Nope! I'm sure I can handle it." Elastigirl

pushed through the lobby doors. The street in front of the theater was packed. *One of the other movies must have just let out,* she realized. She was surrounded by a crowd of people trying to avoid getting wet.

"Watch out!" she cried, ducking and weaving to avoid being impaled by multiple umbrellas. She had no idea what the crime was or which way she should go. And the area was so packed she couldn't see a thing!

She *s-t-r-e-c-h-e-d* her neck and wiggled it up through the canopy of umbrellas. Rain poured down on her as she turned her head in all directions above the sea of plastic. Then she spotted something amiss. A horse and carriage were careening down the street. A skinny man with a ponytail sat on the driver's bench, tugging on the reins. The horse looked frantic and the carriage swung wildly from side to side, in danger of toppling with every movement. "Oh, no," she murmured.

Elastigirl wondered why the driver couldn't manage his own horse and carriage. Had something spooked the horse?

She got her answer a moment later. A man in a top hat raced along the sidewalk shouting, "He stole my horse and carriage! Stop him!"

Elastigirl started wading through umbrellas once more. "Ow, ow, ow!" she yelped as umbrellas poked her lengthened neck. She retracted her head, only now she couldn't see anything. She was too hemmed in.

"Excuse me, pardon me, excuse me," she said, trying to weave through the crowd. No one would move. "Fine," she muttered. She dropped down and flattened herself, then wriggled and wiggled through the forest of legs like a Super snake.

"Phew!" she exhaled as she broke free from the group. She stood and stretched her neck above the umbrellas again. The horse was still galloping down the street, sending pedestrians flinging themselves onto the curb and causing cars to swerve dangerously. The driver was clinging desperately to the seat.

The rightful owner stood nearby, wringing his hands. "My poor Sophie. If he harms my horse . . . !"

"Don't worry," Elastigirl told him. "I'll have

Sophie back to you lickety-split!" With that, she stretched her legs and raced after the speeding carriage.

Just then, a large car screeched around the corner. It instantly pulled ahead of her, then drove up just behind the carriage.

Elastigirl pumped her legs as fast as they could go, her eyes trained on the runaway carriage and the car tailing it. At that moment, Mr. Incredible leaned out the car's window, one hand still on the steering wheel. With the other, he grabbed hold of the back of the carriage.

"Look, it's Mr. Incredible in his Incredibile!" someone shouted.

"Wow, Mr. Incredible?"

"Neat!"

More and more bystanders gathered to watch the chase, spilling onto the rainy street and blocking Elastigirl's way.

"Gah!" she cried, slowing to a stop. She started to push through more umbrella-bearing passersby, but then thought better of it. She knew she could spook the horse and interfere with Mr.

Incredible's plan if she ran up to them. Stretching her neck again so she could get a better look, she watched, waiting to see if her help was needed.

Meanwhile, Mr. Incredible pumped the brakes, forcing the horse to strain against the weight of his car. The horse let out a whinny and slowly trotted to a stop. The horse thief leapt from the driver's seat.

"Oh, no, you don't!" Mr. Incredible shouted. He quickly released the carriage, clambered out of the car, and then thundered after the man. The horse nickered and went to chew on a potted plant in front of a store.

Mr. Incredible snatched the man by his shirt collar. "What were you thinking, stealing a horse-drawn carriage when you don't know how to drive one?" he demanded. Mr. Incredible held the man up to his face. The man seemed to shrink into his clothes.

"I didn't think it would be so hard," the man admitted in a small voice.

Mr. Incredible shook his head. "That's the problem with you criminals. You just don't think things through." Mr. Incredible strolled to the carriage and patted the horse. Then he turned to face the crowd. "Nothing to worry about now, folks. It's all under control!"

The crowd let out a cheer as Elastigirl brought her head back down to her shoulders. *Great. Mr. Incredible got the bad guy.*

And all she could do was stand there, getting rained on and being poked by umbrellas.

CHAPTER 6

A week or so later, Elastigirl shivered in the chill wind. It wasn't raining anymore, but the night had turned cold. A cat yowled nearby. She could just make out its arched back and puffed tail high atop the wire fence in the moonlight.

After the less-than-ideal circumstances of the runaway carriage incident, she had been looking forward to a case she could really sink her teeth into. And boy, did she have one now!

"Come on, come on, come on," she murmured from her position, lying on the pavement underneath a truck. She was on a stakeout at an Elwin's Electronics warehouse, keeping an eye on the loading dock. Dicker had assigned her to put the location under surveillance for the past week.

Expensive electronics had been going missing from the chain's various facilities in the tristate area. The NSA was working with local law enforcement and had intel that Municiberg was where the criminal ringleader had his operations. Word on the street was this particular warehouse was going to be hit. Tonight.

Elastigirl scanned the area. It was just before midnight: the time when most criminal dealings went down, in Elastigirl's experience. And sure enough . . . *Bingo.* An unmarked van rumbled into the lot and up to the loading dock. Three people dressed in black, all wearing ski masks to cover their faces, hurried out of the van and up the steps. Someone pulled out a key ring so big Elastigirl could hear it jangling from her spot under the truck.

The thieves were in and out of the warehouse quickly. Clearly they were working with someone on the inside, someone who could get them keys and knew where the good stuff was kept. Each thief was pushing a pallet piled with stereos, televisions, and even super-fancy lighting fixtures.

Working in near silence, they loaded up the van and drove off.

None of them knew Elastigirl had caught hold of the van's bumper and was now clinging to the back. She had no intention of stopping them. She was after bigger prey. She was after the big cheese, the one in charge.

Elastigirl slithered up to the roof of the van and flattened herself so no one would be able to see her. She didn't want some passing driver or bystander panicking and warning the thieves that there was someone attached to their van. She clutched the sides of the van's roof and held on as it sped toward the wharf.

She stayed low as the thieves drove up to the parking lot of another enormous warehouse—the old fishing warehouse, by the looks of it. A faded sign displayed the outline of a cartoon fish. The windows were boarded up and the paint was peeling. In fact, it seemed to be abandoned.

Except, she realized, for the other identical vans parked in the lot.

The thieves climbed out of the van and

unloaded their stolen goods. They wheeled the pallets to the warehouse door. One of them knocked a signal: Three times. Pause. Twice. Pause. Once.

Then they waited.

The doors slowly screeched open. They entered, and the doors slammed back into place.

Elastigirl waited a moment, then slid off the roof of the van. She stayed low and crept to the parked vans. She stretched her neck just high enough to peek into each window.

All empty. So she only had to worry about whoever was inside the warehouse. And how many of them there were.

Elastigirl stretched her legs and crossed the lot in two steps. Then she flattened herself like a pancake and slid under the warehouse door.

Everyone was too busy examining the latest haul to pay any attention to her. She slithered to a standing position in a shadowy corner.

In the center of the room, a small man with a large mustache sat at a table. Behind him were old fishing rods and nets, along with shelves stacked with what Elastigirl surmised was more stolen equipment. Men and women brought items for him to inspect, and once he approved, they loaded up the shelves.

She'd done it. Elastigirl had found the ringleader. Normally, the NSA wanted Supers to call for backup when there was a good number of criminals in one place. Only she couldn't risk calling this in. The warehouse was too quiet. She'd have to handle it on her own.

She took in her surroundings. It looked like once the deliveries of stolen goods were made, the thieves who'd brought them settled into chairs just outside the spill of bright light on the ringleader's table. From what she could see, there was only the one entrance. Surprisingly, no one seemed to be armed.

That was a very good thing.

One of me, Elastigirl thought, *six of them. Plus the dude in charge.*

She grinned.

No problem.

She slid down the wall and flattened herself on the floor. She slithered along the dark outer edges of the warehouse as if she were a traveling puddle. She kept her eyes peeled for anything that could be useful as she wriggled toward the chairs where three thieves sat.

A coil of rope rested beside a toolbox on the bottom shelf she was passing. *That'll work.*

She pulled the rope along with her as she continued to move, snakelike, along the floor. Gently, carefully, silently she wrapped the rope around the legs of the metal folding chairs.

One, two... she mouthed silently. "Three!" She yanked on the rope hard, jerking the three chairs backward. The thieves landed hard, leaving them dazed. Elastigirl quickly tied them up.

"What's going on?" the ringleader shouted, knocking back his own chair as he stood. The three thieves sitting on the other side of the warehouse also scrambled to their feet.

Elastigirl leapt up and vaulted across the room. She executed a somersault and shot out her leg as she uncurled. Her foot connected with the jaw of one of the thieves. Down he went. She landed and immediately jumped up again, corkscrewing her legs and kicking the other two thieves in the heads, one after the other. They flew backwards as she landed again.

The ringleader lunged for her with a shout. She spun and grabbed his shoulders. Using her stretch, she held him far enough away from herself that his blows couldn't reach her. She wound her other stretched arm around the necks of the three thieves as they came at her, stringing them together.

"Help!" a thief choked out, clutching at the arm that was wrapped around his neck. "Help!"

"You helped yourself already," Elastigirl said. "To other people's electronics."

Still holding the ringleader's shoulders, she knocked his feet out from under him with a well-aimed kick as she simultaneously released him. He landed with a thud and was knocked unconscious.

"Quit squirming," she told the thieves she had tied together with her stretched arm. "It won't hurt as much." She was glad her Supersuit was scratchproof as they clawed at her, trying to get away. With her other hand, she tapped a button on her headband.

"NSA? Elastigirl here. I got 'em."

After giving the address of the warehouse, she clicked off. Moments later, the cops arrived with an NSA escort and hauled the thieves away.

Elastigirl stepped back out into the night and took a deep breath of the cool air.

"Job well done," she told herself. There was no one else around to say it.

CHAPTER 7

"Elastigirl, you've been nursing that soda awhile." Frozone swiveled around on his stool to face her. It was a few days after her Elwin's Electronics assignment. When Elastigirl had gotten home that night, before taking her usual warm bath to ease her stretched muscles, she'd noticed another letter from the NSA—this one an invitation to the opening of the brand-new headquarters for Blazestone and Universal Man's team, Beta Force.

Now she and Frozone were hanging out at the ice cream shop located inside.

"Probably warm by now. Let me take care of that for you." Frozone gripped her soda glass, and instantly, frost coated its surface.

“Thanks, Frozone.” Elastigirl sipped on her straw. Her brows knit together and she tried again. Nothing. “Uh, I think you overdid it.” She held out her glass. The soda inside was frozen solid.

Frozone chuckled. “Sorry ’bout that! I’ll go grab you another.” He leapt over the counter and took a glass off the back shelf. Then he picked up the soda gun and filled the glass. He slid it across the counter to her.

“Thanks.” Elastigirl sipped through the straw. “I do like my liquids, you know . . . *liquid*.”

“I hear that.” Frozone scooped out some vanilla ice cream and plunked it into a sundae dish. He squirted a hefty portion of chocolate sauce all over it. A bright red cherry on top completed the treat. Frozone licked his lips as he rummaged in a drawer for a spoon.

“Isn’t that your third sundae?” Elastigirl asked.

Frozone laughed. “Need to keep the chill going on.” He took a big spoonful of his ice cream. “I’m so glad they decided to put in this ice cream shop. Ice cream *is* my favorite food group.”

Amused, Elastigirl shook her head and spun around to check out the scene. The NSA had just finished refurbishing the space for Beta Force, so everything felt new and shiny. At the moment it resembled a rec center for Supers more than a crime-fighting team's home base. The enormous space had been a pavilion for the Municiberg World's Fair that had taken place more than twenty years before. Now the abandoned structure housed not only the latest in crime-fighting equipment—and the ice cream shop where Frozone and Elastigirl were having their treats—but also game tables, a basketball court, a library, and lots of nooks for sitting, chatting, and crafting. She spotted four Supers working together sewing a large colorful quilt.

Elastigirl suspected the NSA had made the new headquarters so lavish and inviting as a way to encourage more camaraderie among the Supers. After all, the place was awfully big for a team of two! She supposed if they hung out more together when they were off the clock, it could lead to better teamwork when they were out in the field.

As she looked around, she noticed all wore their Supersuits and masks. Elastigirl realized she didn't know most of their secret identities, and many didn't know hers. The NSA had been growing in the last few years, with a lot more Supers arriving in Municiberg. If she ran into some of them when she was out and about as Helen Highwater, they'd never know it. And she wouldn't recognize them, either. There were some she hadn't even met as Supers yet.

But there were some recognizable Supers in the crowd, too; she saw Apogee's pale blue suit with the pointy shoulders over by the pinball machine. Her opponent was Gamma Jack. Elastigirl knew that several of the Supers referred to him as "Handsome Jack" behind his back. He had quite a reputation as a ladies' man. Sure, his thick blond swoop of hair, sharp nose, and square jaw could be viewed as attractive, but he was so not Elastigirl's type. Much too into hair products and mirrors.

And it was easy to spot the newest NSA recruit, Downburst. His yellow cape fluttered as he dribbled a basketball down the court, and his bald head was shiny under the bright lights.

Gazerbeam raced down the court after him,

trying to block Downburst's attempt to sink a basket. He was Apogee's former partner as part of the now-disbanded team, the Thrilling Three. This was one Super whose secret identity Elastigirl knew: he was a pro bono lawyer. She recalled that once there had been a conflict of interest: Gazerbeam had caught a criminal by shooting out intense laser blasts through his energy-focusing visor. The next day, after trading in his burgundy Supersuit for a lawyerly suit and tie, he was assigned to defend the very same criminal in court. The NSA had had to get involved.

Watching him dribble the basketball away from Downburst, Elastigirl wondered what had ever happened to the Thrilling Three's mode of transport, the Thrilling Three Chopper. The custom-designed motorcycle had had two side-cars. *Must have been difficult to maneuver in traffic,* she thought. *And really tough to park.*

Elastigirl turned back around and took another sip of her very cold soda. She grinned at Frozone. She could always find her friend in the crowd. Even if she didn't see his kind face or bright snow-colored suit, she'd recognize the way he moved—with the elegance of an Olympic downhill skier.

"Point and match!" a woman shouted gleefully, catching Elastigirl's attention.

Elastigirl glanced over to the Ping-Pong table set up nearby. Blazestone was waving her hands over her head, chanting, "I'm a winner. You're a loser. I'm a winner. You're a loser!"

Blazestone's opponent—and crime-fighting partner—Universal Man folded his arms across his chest and fumed. "You are going to forfeit the game by displaying poor sportsmanship," he said. "This is *not* the way to behave."

Blazestone twirled her paddle. "Aw, come on. I'm just joking around. It's only a game."

Now that Elastigirl was observing so many Supers together, she realized that Blazestone's midnight-blue suit was the only one with short sleeves. She thought it must be because Blazestone's power involved fire and heated air, and often sent out sparks. She'd need to keep herself cool somehow. She probably wore her blond hair in a high ponytail for the same reason.

“How one plays a game speaks volumes,” Universal Man lectured. “And your attitude is not seemly.”

“Sheesh. Lighten up.”

Elastigirl swiveled her stool back around, turning her back on the argument. “That is not a match made in heaven,” she said to Frozone, who was now squirting whipped cream from a can onto his sundae. She tipped her head to indicate Blazestone and Universal Man. “What was the NSA thinking, putting those two together?”

“They were probably thinking about Blazestone’s criminal past,” Frozone said.

Elastigirl gaped at him. “Seriously?” She turned and took another look at Blazestone. Universal Man had stomped away, and Blazestone was now playing Ping-Pong with Gazerbeam.

“Yeah, keep that quiet, though. It’s not really common knowledge,” Frozone said. “They only told me because I was her first partner.”

Elastigirl shook her head. Now she was even happier she had turned down that team-leader spot. Relieved, even. And now that she thought about it, this backstory kind of made sense. Blazestone seemed more rebellious than most.

"Universal Man is a big stickler for rules," Frozone said. "The NSA probably figured there was no one better to keep her in check."

"Maybe her criminal past is why she's been so successful at apprehending bad guys," Elastigirl suggested. "She knows how they think."

"Could be," Frozone mused. "She's definitely doing her part to make Municiberg safe. She has been bringing in the villains." He took another spoonful of his ice cream sundae. "I only mentioned her past because I figured you already knew. I heard they offered you leadership of Beta Force and would have been supervising her."

"I won't confirm or deny," Elastigirl said. She was only just getting to know Blazestone. She didn't want things to be awkward between them, and that could happen if Blazestone knew the NSA had planned on putting Elastigirl in charge of her team.

Frozone studied her. "I take it you said no."

"I won't confirm or deny," Elastigirl said again.

Frozone smirked. "Okay, let me ask a different way. How come you've *never* accepted a team leadership?" he asked her. "I know you've been offered a spot more than once."

Elastigirl shrugged and stirred her soda with her straw. "I'd rather work alone."

"Well, I can appreciate that, being unaffiliated myself," Frozone said, "but I have to say, I do like it when Mr. Incredible and I work together from time to time."

"Yeah?" Elastigirl asked.

"We get into a flow, a rhythm, when we best the bad guys. Like singing in harmony. Or those two being so good at working as a pair."

He pointed, and Elastigirl twirled on her stool to face the game tables. Apogee had left the pinball machine and was now playing partnered badminton with Downburst. Universal Man had joined them, paired with Everseer.

Elastigirl could see immediately that Apogee and Downburst were working in sync and that Everseer and Universal Man definitely were not. Apogee would go high; Downburst would go low.

Apogee stepped back when Downburst moved forward. Each got out of the other's way to make points.

Everseer and Universal Man were another story. They banged into each other as they each dove for the shuttlecock, making them miss the point. Or neither would move and then both would complain, "I thought *you* were going to hit it."

"You'd think with Everseer's telepathic abilities he'd be better at anticipating his partner's moves," Elastigirl commented.

"You'd think," Frozone agreed. "I suspect it's because neither he nor Universal Man thinks of the other *as* a partner. They may be playing doubles, but they're acting as if they're playing as singles."

It didn't help that after each play, Everseer would stop and use the hand sanitizer he kept stashed at the sidelines on his hands and on his racket. He was a terrible germophobe. It was a good thing his power was mental. That was one Super who did not want to get up close and personal with, well, *anyone*. Probably because he could see down to the microscopic level. Every germ and microbe on any surface was visible to him. *He would have been paralyzed by that spilled garbage the other day,* Elastigirl thought, *and Mysterious Melvin might have gotten away.*

"I get what you're saying," Elastigirl said as Everseer threw his racket to the ground in frustration. "And if it works for you, fine and dandy. But I'm a solo kind of gal."

Unsurprisingly, Apogee and Downburst won the game. Apogee grinned and waved when she saw Elastigirl. She and Downburst put away their rackets and strolled over to the ice cream shop.

"I could use one of those," Downburst said, eyeing Elastigirl's drink. He hopped behind the bar and started fiddling with the soda gun. A blast of soda shot out, nearly hitting Apogee and Elastigirl, who ducked out of the way.

"Gah! Sorry!" Downburst cried.

"You're bringing a whole new meaning to the term 'soda jerk,'" Apogee joked.

"No harm done," Elastigirl said, stretching her arm out to reach for a rag on the other side of the counter and wiping off the wall.

Frozone helped Downburst adjust the soda gun. "It's just like anything. Takes a few tries to get into your... *element*." He laughed, creating some ice cubes from the water molecules in the air and tossing them into Downburst's glass before Downburst filled it.

"Thanks," the new Super murmured.

"No problem," Frozone said.

"I'm in the mood for a hot chocolate," Gamma Jack announced as he and Everseer joined them. "Is there anything like that back there?"

"I think I can take care of that for you," Apogee said. She slid behind the counter. Using her suit's stored solar power, she heated up a mug of cold milk, then added chocolate syrup. "With or without whipped cream?"

"Without," Gamma Jack said. "But I *will* take some toasted marshmallows."

"You got it." Apogee pulled some mini-marshmallows out of a bin and plopped them into the mug. She held a finger above each little pillowy marshmallow until it was a golden brown. She dropped in a spoon. "Ta-da!"

"Thanks." Gamma Jack stirred the hot chocolate. Elastigirl saw steam rising.

"I saw your Supers Appreciation Day eight-by-ten glossy photos," Downburst told Gamma Jack, twirling his straw in his soda. "They look good."

Handsome Gamma Jack ran a hand through his thick hair. "Yeah, I told the NSA to order a thousand. Might not be enough, though. I do have a lot of fans, and they're all going to want autographed pics."

"Is everyone handing out pictures and giving autographs?" Elastigirl asked.

"I'm not," said Everseer. "It all seems a little too–"

"Fun?" Gamma Jack said.

Everseer narrowed his eyes at Gamma Jack, who laughed. "I was going to say *silly*," Everseer said. "And all those germs from contact with fans." He shuddered.

"I think it's going to be exciting," Downburst said. "Municiberg's very first Supers Appreciation Day! There's going to be so much to do. It'll be like a big party!"

"Better not be any villains around *that* day!" Elastigirl quipped. "We'll all be too busy taking fan photos and judging best costume to do any crime-fighting!"

Everyone laughed, but it occurred to Elastigirl that maybe it wasn't actually funny. It *would* be the perfect day for a serious crime spree. She made a mental note to discuss the possibility with Rick Dicker at the NSA.

A few more Supers stepped up to the ice cream shop counter, so Elastigirl relinquished her stool. She carried her soda over to the library and flopped into a cozy armchair. Flipping his yellow cape over one shoulder, Downburst settled into the armchair next to hers.

"Are you looking forward to marching in the Supers parade?" Downburst asked.

"Oh, right, the parade," Elastigirl responded. This Supers Appreciation Day was far more involved than she'd realized. *I guess I should have been paying more attention during that briefing,* she thought.

"Yes!" Downburst replied. "From town hall to the band shell by the pier. The band shell is where the costume contest and the awards ceremony will be."

“Ah!” Elastigirl drained the last of her soda and stretched out her arm all the way back to the ice cream shop. She placed the empty glass on the counter, then retracted her arm again.

“I can’t believe the NSA included me in the parade,” Downburst said.

“Why?” Elastigirl asked.

Downburst twirled the straw in his soda, suddenly shy. “Oh, I don’t know. . . . I mean, my powers are still developing.”

Elastigirl patted his arm. “Most of us had to work on our powers. Everyone starts somewhere. What have you been doing in training?”

“Lots of things. Mostly atom-manipulating experiments. What I’m struggling with a bit is keeping focused during an actual crime. I get distracted.”

“It happens. That’s what training is for: to practice under all different circumstances.”

“You’ve always been so nice to me,” Downburst said. “It’s taken a while for some of the Supers to accept me.”

“Manipulating atoms is an impressive ability,” Elastigirl assured him.

"I suppose. And I know that being able to heal small wounds comes in handy—"

"Of course it does!"

"But I want to be able to do more."

"That's why you're training," Elastigirl said. "So you'll be able to be all you can be!"

Downburst smiled and Elastigirl noticed he had dimples. The guy was so shy, this was probably the first time she'd seen him grin so broadly.

"I *am* testing out some of my new skills of matter manipulation," Downburst confided. "And it's pretty promising, if I do say so myself."

"Can you tell me about it?" Elastigirl asked.

He leaned forward. "Bicycles."

"Huh?"

"I'm experimenting with making bicycles. All different shapes and sizes."

"That sounds... interesting." She wasn't exactly sure if bicycles were something Supers would be impressed by, but she wanted to encourage him. "You keep working on that. And if you want, I'm happy to give you some feedback."

"Really?" Downburst's eyes widened behind his mask. "You'd do that?"

"Sure! I'd help a Super out."

Suddenly, Downburst looked down at his drink. He seemed to shrink a little, and his bald head turned a slight pink.

Is he *blushing*? Elastigirl glanced around, trying to figure out what—or who—was causing him to react this way.

Blazestone strolled by and Downburst sighed again. "I'll never be in her league," he said wistfully. "She apprehended three criminals just today! No wonder she ignores me."

Aha. So Downburst had a crush on Blazestone. "You're just as good as she is," Elastigirl assured him.

"Have you heard anything about ZAP?" Downburst asked suddenly.

"That radioactive stuff the NSA is experimenting with? Yeah, why?"

"I wonder if it would help me develop my powers more quickly."

"Hate to interrupt," Mr. Incredible cut in, coming up behind Elastigirl's chair.

"But you will anyway," Elastigirl muttered. She wondered how long he had been standing there. And when he had arrived at Beta Force headquarters. She hadn't noticed him before.

"I couldn't help overhearing." Mr. Incredible perched his large form on the arm of Elastigirl's overstuffed armchair. He put a hand on the arm of Downburst's and leaned in toward the bashful Super. "Never touch that stuff. All natural is always better."

Elastigirl had to admit she agreed with him.

"Quick fixes are usually a bad idea," Mr. Incredible continued. He looked down at Elastigirl. "Am I right?"

She nodded. "If it seems too good to be true, it usually is."

Just then, her crime alert went off. She heard buzzes and bells all around the room. Instantly, Supers sprang into action, tossing aside rackets and spilling sodas. The Supers in the crafts section dropped knitting needles, glue guns, and glitter.

Blazestone shouted, "Don't worry! I'll handle it!" She disappeared out the door on a whoosh of heated air.

"Wait for me!" Universal Man yelled as he

lifted off the ground and flew after her. "We're supposed to be partners!"

Mr. Incredible stood and cupped his hands around his mouth. "Hey, Frozone!" he shouted.

"Yeah, Mr. I?" Frozone called back from the ice cream shop.

"Why should we let those two have all the fun?"

Frozone shot some canned whipped cream into his mouth, then leapt over the counter. He and Mr. Incredible met at the door.

"Ready?" Frozone and Mr. Incredible asked each other simultaneously.

"Always!" they replied together, then cracked up laughing. They ran off, too.

Downburst was craning his neck, watching all the activity.

"Hey! Here's your chance to strut your stuff," Elastigirl told him.

He faced her again and brightened, his dimples reappearing. "I can try out my latest villain-apprehension lesson in the real world. Not just hypothetical."

“Right! Work on that focus!” She grinned as Downburst hustled away, his yellow cape flapping behind him.

Elastigirl started to settle back into the comfy chair, then sat bolt upright. “Wait a sec!” She smacked her forehead. “There’s a crime in progress! I’d better go, too!”

She dashed out of the Beta Force headquarters, stretching her legs as she ran.

CHAPTER 8

Once outside Beta Force headquarters, Elastigirl kept stretching her legs until she could peer over the nearby buildings. She spotted some Supers running on foot and others flying through the air. Up ahead, Frozone continually threw out ice, creating a frozen pathway to surf along. Mr. Incredible drove underneath him in his Incredibile, his souped-up car outfitted with all kinds of villain-catching equipment. Elastigirl still had no idea what crime was going down, but it seemed to be happening in the park. That was the direction all the Supers were heading.

She could have just left it to the others to solve. After all, dozens of Supers were on the case. But she wasn't that kind of gal. Besides, the situation might require her very special powers. So she stalked the streets, keeping her eyes peeled for . . . whatever.

When Elastigirl arrived in the park, she discovered what had set off the crime signal alerts. A gang of ruffians was using oversized fans and fast motorboats to create massive waves in the lake. People shrieked and screamed and ran for cover. Kids wailed as their toy boats toppled over.

"But why?" she murmured. "Just to be mean?" Sometimes scaring people was the sole purpose behind a perpetrator's actions. Those villains were the ones that angered her the most. But as she watched, she understood. These guys actually had some kind of plan in mind.

The waves the gang whipped up were tipping over rowboats, sending their occupants splashing into the lake. And as the artificial fan-generated waves crashed onto the shore, people who had been sitting there dashed away. Then the ruffians struck. They rushed to grab whatever was left behind on the shore. And, Elastigirl realized, anything that fell out of the boats was scooped up in their gigantic nets.

They're using the water to send everyone running and then stealing the stuff left behind! Elastigirl fumed.

She quickly sized up the situation, looking for the Supers who had already made it to the scene. She noticed Blazestone arguing with Universal Man on the other side of the lake. *Must have a difference of opinion about how to proceed,* Elastigirl thought. That was the problem with partners. If you don't agree on what to do, how can you do anything?

Downburst was at the edge of the lake, desperately trying to shift the atoms in the waves but only managing to get drenched. He didn't seem to be in any danger, though, so Elastigirl concentrated on coming up with her own plan.

Digging her feet into the wet dirt at the edge of the lake, she started to stretch her body to form a canopy. Her idea was to contain the waves and trap the ruffians inside, putting an end to their nonsense.

Leaves and branches tangled in her hair as her head reached the tree line. She pulled them away and prepared to do her massive bend over the lake. Then she spotted Frozone and Mr. Incredible below her.

Frozone zipped around the lake, freezing the water and trapping the gang's motorboats among the ice floes. Meanwhile, Mr. Incredible quickly smashed the fans, putting an end to the disruptive wave-making.

"Ready, Mr. I?" Frozone called.

"Ready, Fro!" Mr. Incredible called back.

Elastigirl watched as the gang members scrambled out of the stalled boats, slipping and sliding along the now-frozen lake. Frozone scooted around them, sending them directly to where Mr. Incredible was waiting. The Supers looked like hockey players, Frozone using the bad guys as pucks and Mr. Incredible the goalie. Using one gang member's giant nets, Mr. Incredible scooped up each hooligan, then tossed him onto a growing heap of his fellow petty crooks.

"We gotcha! Oh, yeah!" Frozone and Mr. Incredible chanted together. "We gotcha! Oh, yeah!"

With all the baddies lying stunned and dazed, Frozone skated an icy victory lap around the lake.

He passed Mr. Incredible and they gave each other a high five.

"Okay, let's get these belongings back to where they belong!" Mr. Incredible shouted. He grabbed another net from the shore beside him and tossed it to Frozone. Together they collected the stolen items while the police arrived to arrest the criminals.

Huh. Elastigirl retracted back to her regular size. Unlike with the runaway carriage incident, she wasn't quite as miffed by the fact that she hadn't been the one to stop the crime this time. If anything, she was impressed. Their approach was different from her own, but Frozone was right—he and Mr. Incredible made a great team. Even if they weren't *officially* partners.

It must be because they're such good friends, she decided. They had an ease together. They were able to anticipate each other's moves. Like a well-oiled machine, they worked smoothly and effectively.

"See what you did?" Elastigirl turned to see Blazestone shouting at Universal Man. "If we'd just done it my way, we would have added six more criminals to our list! Don't you even *want* that award?"

Moving quickly, Elastigirl walked by them, making sure not to even cast a glance in their direction. She didn't want to get pulled into the middle of *that* argument.

Blazestone shouldn't be so angry, Elastigirl thought. Sure, it was frustrating when someone else got the collar. But most important was that everyone was okay and the ruffians had been stopped.

Elastigirl was about to make her way back to Beta Force headquarters when she noticed there was another Super still at the scene. Downburst stood at the edge of the lake, shoulders slumped, suit drenched. Drawing back her shoulders, Elastigirl strode toward him. She had a feeling his self-confidence was going to need a little more boosting.

She might not have had a hand in apprehending the bad guys this time . . . but she could certainly do something to help one of the good ones.

CHAPTER 9

The next morning, Elastigirl stood with other Supers in front of town hall in downtown Municiberg, waiting for Rick Dicker to begin the Supers Appreciation Day briefing. She stretched her neck to check out the assembled group. This was the first time there had been an official meeting bringing all the active Supers in the area together.

She brought her neck back to its normal length and shifted from side to side impatiently. The notice said the meeting could take at least an hour. *At least!* What if there was a crime being committed somewhere? On top of that, she had laundry to do.

Finally! Rick Dicker shambled to the podium

that had been set up at the top of the wide town hall steps. Shirley strode along behind him in another one of her patented colorful outfits, this one a striped chartreuse-and-lime pantsuit with a bright pillbox hat, her pointy heels clicking loudly on the marble.

"Thank you all for coming," Dicker's gravelly voice boomed through the microphone. He looked startled by the loud sound and glanced to Shirley. She stepped up beside him and made an adjustment on the microphone. He gave her a sharp nod as thanks, then faced the assembled Supers again.

He shuffled some papers on the podium and began reading from them. "'The NSA would like to express its appreciation for your participation in the very first Municiberg Supers Appreciation Day. We at the NSA hope that it will become an annual event. It is part of our continual campaign to connect with the community at large. Maintaining the goodwill and support of the people is essential to our efforts.'"

"Shouldn't they just appreciate what we do

without throwing a party and insisting we attend?" Blazestone muttered. Elastigirl's eyes flicked to the Super. She was surprised to hear Blazestone shared her opinion. Maybe all the hoopla surrounding the event was making Universal Man even more difficult for the rebellious Super to deal with. Elastigirl could see how that might make her cranky.

Dicker put aside his notes. "So today we'll go over the logistics. First there will be a screening of the cartoon film *Mr. Incredible and Friends* here at the town hall."

"All right!" Mr. Incredible cheered from the back of the crowd amidst a smattering of applause.

They made a movie about him? Elastigirl turned to see Mr. Incredible. A few Supers were clapping him on the back, and Gamma Jack was shaking his hand. Meanwhile, Blazestone didn't seem to be paying attention, rifling through a notebook instead. Elastigirl couldn't blame her. Mr. Incredible had an ego *now*. It would balloon to the size of a dirigible if that movie was a success. Elastigirl turned to face Dicker again.

"After the film—" Dicker began, but Mr. Incredible interrupted him.

"Will there be a Q and A after the screening?" Mr. Incredible asked.

Dicker's brows knit together over his horn-rimmed glasses. He glanced to Shirley. She consulted her clipboard and shook her head no.

"There will not be," Dicker said.

"How about an autograph session for the stars of the movie?" Mr. Incredible asked.

Elastigirl rolled her eyes.

Dicker's eyes shot to Shirley again, who this time mouthed the word *no*.

"No," Dicker said.

"But—" Mr. Incredible began, but this time Dicker cut off the Super.

"May I proceed with the briefing? We can answer all questions at the band shell. I believe the mayor would like us to clear out of the way so he can get his day started at the town hall."

Elastigirl swiveled her head, twisting her stretchy neck in order to see the street behind her. They mayor's black limo was just pulling up.

Mr. Incredible held up his hands. "Of course, of

course . . . I was only thinking of the people. You know, give the public what they want."

"The NSA appreciates your enthusiasm," Dicker said drily. "And now, we will walk the parade route along Main Street to the pier."

The Supers followed Dicker and Shirley through the streets. Elastigirl watched as many chattered excitedly about the upcoming event. She just couldn't get herself to be so unreservedly enthusiastic about it. It just seemed like so much . . . fuss.

The sea air tickled Elastigirl's nose when they arrived at the wharf. The band shell stood at the end of the largest pier. Elastigirl had attended several concerts there, though lately she'd been so busy fighting crime that she'd missed a few.

Rick Dicker and Shirley climbed the few steps onto the band shell stage. Another podium had been set up in front of it. Elastigirl wondered how much longer this meeting was going to last.

"The parade will culminate here," Rick Dicker said when he took his position at the podium.

"We're going to need to be able to stop along the parade route," Mr. Incredible called out.

"Why is that?" Dicker asked.

"Fans will demand it," Mr. Incredible explained. "They'll stop us for autographs. For photo ops." He shrugged. "After all, this is the closest many of them will get to a Super."

"Unless they're the victim of a crime," Apogee said.

"Or a criminal," Blazestone added, her focus back on the briefing. The two Supers giggled.

Mr. Incredible took their teasing in stride and smiled. "You know what I'm saying. I'm just thinking of the fans."

Yeah, right. Elastigirl rolled her eyes. Every time she started to see a different, more positive side of Mr. Incredible, like his give-and-take with Frozone and their awesome friendship, he'd say something that reminded her he was all about his ego. She saw her abilities as a Super as a way to be of service. He seemed to think they were a way to be a star.

"Okay," Dicker said. "Shirley, make a note that the parade will probably last longer than we have it currently scheduled."

Shirley scribbled on her clipboard.

"All right then," Dicker continued. "After the

parade, we will begin the costume contest. Who are my judges?"

Gazerbeam, Gamma Jack, and Apogee raised their hands.

"Make a note," Dicker said.

Shirley made a note.

"There will be seating set aside in the bleachers that will be for Supers only. And the area on the pier behind the band shell will also be accessible only by those with the same passes we'll be giving you for the bleachers. Shirley?"

Shirley held up a lanyard. A laminated card dangled from it. Even from her spot in the middle of the group, Elastigirl could read the large blue letters: ALL-ACCESS PASS.

"Official contestants will have these, too. They will be the only non-Supers allowed behind the band shell. Other than the security team, of course."

"That's a lot of All-Access Passes to hand out," Frozone commented.

"We will be checking them very carefully," Dicker assured him. "They will only get into the hands of those who should have them. I believe that's all."

Thank goodness. Elastigirl turned to leave.

"Ahem," said Shirley, clearing her throat.

"Oh, yes. Shirley will brief you on the other . . . festivities."

Elastigirl sighed and turned back to face the stage again.

Shirley stepped up to the microphone, adjusting her vibrant hat. She consulted her clipboard. "As everyone is getting into place for the costume contest, the Municiberg High School band will play. They'll be down here." She waved at the area just below the band shell stage. "The judges will have a table over there." She pointed to the center front row of the Supers section of the bleachers. "The contestants will march across the stage. Universal Man will introduce them."

"You're welcome," Universal Man said.

Shirley shot him a look but continued. "Once the contest is over and the winner chosen, the band will play again. That will let us get ready for the Supers Awards ceremony. The Criminals Caught numbers will be tallied, as will the votes for Fan Favorite, during the presentation of the awards for Most Improved, Friendliest, and Most Promising Newcomer."

An excited buzz ran through the gathered group. Clearly there were many Supers who were really looking forward to Supers Appreciation Day and the awards.

It just wasn't Elastigirl's style. She'd rather just focus on her job. And did she really want to spend an entire day marching and posing for pictures and then waiting around to see who won the awards? *Especially,* she thought, her eyes flicking to Universal Man and Mr. Incredible, *since there are bound to be a few sore losers.*

"You can't keep striking out on your own," Universal Man whispered hoarsely to Blazestone.

"Taking initiative, you mean," Blazestone retorted.

"We've talked about this before," Universal Man groused.

"*You've* talked about it," Blazestone said, gesturing with her notebook.

"If you would *listen*—" Universal Man began.

"Oh, give it a rest, rooster head," Blazestone snapped.

Elastigirl bit her lip to keep from laughing. Now that Blazestone said it, the three peaks on Universal Man's red helmet did kind of resemble a rooster's comb.

"Ah-*hem*." Shirley scanned the group to try to identify who was interrupting her explanation of the costume contest rules. Elastigirl shifted a few inches so Shirley wouldn't think she was part of the Blazestone–Universal Man argument. An argument the Beta Force team seemed to always be having.

Blazestone has a point, Elastigirl thought. *Her crime-fighting streak has been impressive.* She probably felt that Universal Man was cramping her style. Elastigirl could relate. She'd probably go nuts herself if she was on a team with Universal Man.

On the other hand, Elastigirl continued musing as Rick Dicker handed out the Supers Appreciation Day schedule, Universal Man wasn't wrong thinking Blazestone was impulsive and often reckless. He probably had the attitude that if they had to be stuck together as a team, they should at least act like one.

Elastigirl shook her head to clear her thoughts.

She could go around and around seeing both sides of their arguments. It was just another sign she was better off "unaffiliated." No team, no problems.

Rick Dicker declared the meeting over and the Supers disbanded. Elastigirl waved goodbye to Frozone, who had stepped over to chat with Mr. Incredible and Apogee. When they saw her they all smiled and waved back. "See you at the parade!" Mr. Incredible called.

Would he? Elastigirl still wasn't sure she wanted to be part of all the hoopla.

Maybe if it's a beautiful day like today, she mused. She strolled along the waterfront, enjoying the lapping of the waves against the piers and the sparkling sunlight reflected on the water. The sky overhead was a bright blue. The birds were singing in the trees. And a woman was screaming that her car had just been stolen.

What? Elastigirl stopped and looked around. She saw a slim woman wearing a pink sweater set and jeans at the corner. A pink handbag swung from the crook of her elbow as she clutched her head and screamed.

"My car! Someone stop him! He stole my car!"

Elastigirl closed the distance between her and the distraught woman in an instant. The bystanders who had gathered made room to allow Elastigirl through.

"What happened, ma'am?" Elastigirl asked.

The woman gripped Elastigirl's arm. "I had just taken my car keys out of my purse when a man ripped them out of my hand, shoved me aside, and drove away."

Elastigirl got a description of the car and the thief. "Stay right here," she told the woman. "Don't worry, I'll get your car back."

She raced in the direction the woman had pointed. "Blue car, 'I Brake for Chocolate' bumper sticker," she repeated, eyes peeled for the vehicle.

Blue car dead ahead! Her feet pounded the street as she ran toward the intersection. The light was changing, but the car sped right through it, nearly getting smashed by a bus. The bus driver let out a loud blast on the horn as Elastigirl launched herself up and over the bus. She landed lightly on the other side, where the car was stopped.

Elastigirl yanked open the driver's side door.

"Where do you think you're going?" she demanded of the driver.

The driver leapt out of his seat, smiling broadly. "In there! My wife is having a baby!"

Elastigirl looked behind her, where the man was pointing. The car had stopped in front of Municiberg Hospital. Still blocking his way, she stretched her neck to check out the back of the car. No bumper stickers. She retracted her head. "Oh. Well, congratulations. But you really shouldn't be speeding."

The man dashed off.

Elastigirl stretched her neck to get a better view of the area. That car could be anywhere by now. But then—*Bingo!*

She was pretty sure she spotted it about ten blocks away. As she watched, the car swerved into an alley. *Is it?* She peered hard. *Yup! There's the bumper sticker.* Elastigirl raced after the car. For the gazillionth time, she wished for a faster form of transportation. Sure, she could clear several streets in a single stretched step, and flipping or even cartwheeling got her around quickly and into difficult-to-reach places. But she still wasn't as fast as Frozone on his ice sheet or Mr. Incredible in his Incredibile.

Or Blazestone on her heated air. Who was already at the car.

Her ability to fly must have been how she beat me here. Elastigirl slowed to a stop and looked for Universal Man. Nope. Blazestone was there on her own. Universal Man wasn't going to be happy about this.

The stolen car was stopped half on, half off the curb. Blazestone must have forced the driver off the street. Good thing there were no pedestrians around to get hurt. The alley was deserted. The driver's side door was open and the engine was still running.

Up ahead, Blazestone seemed to be having a conversation with the thief. *Probably bragging about how many criminals she caught today,* Elastigirl thought. Then she reminded herself that what mattered was the bad guy had been taken out of action and there was no collateral damage.

"Hey! Blazestone!" Elastigirl called as she approached. "Need some help?"

Blazestone looked around, startled. "Elastigirl!"

she exclaimed. The criminal looked more frightened. "Good to see you!"

Blazestone lifted the criminal as she rose several feet off the ground. "I think we understand each other, don't we?" she snarled. The criminal's knees knocked and his face grew pale as he dangled above the street. All he could do was nod.

"Now it's time to get you to the authorities," she told the baddie. She smirked at Elastigirl. "He's not going to give me any trouble."

"Good work," Elastigirl said.

Blazestone winked at her. "Just part of being a Super, right?"

"Right. I'll get the car back to its rightful owner."

"Thanks," Blazestone said. Gripping the criminal's collar tightly, she whooshed away.

Elastigirl slipped behind the wheel of the stolen car. As she drove along, she made a mental note: *talk to Downburst about testing those bicycles, and soon!*

If she had one of those babies, maybe next time she'd beat Blazestone to the crime scene.

CHAPTER 10

Late the next morning, Elastigirl, dressed as Helen Highwater, jogged up the steps of the Municiberg Public Library. She'd been so busy with her crime-stopping and NSA meetings that she had forgotten all about the stack of library books sitting on her bedside table. She hadn't even gotten around to starting them. Oh, well.

She closed her eyes, inhaled the familiar lemonwood-polish scent, and smiled. She always enjoyed the library. It was such a place of calm in an often hectic world. Everyone spoke in soft tones. Books sat neatly on shelves, just waiting to be read. The sun shone through the tall windows, casting a warm glow on the highly polished woodwork. Helen sometimes spent her rare days off relaxing in one of the comfy rocking chairs, reading a thick book. She got in line and waited to have her books checked back in.

"Hi, Helen," the young librarian greeted her from behind the large desk when it was her turn.

"Hi, Roberta," Helen replied, laying her four books on the counter. "I'm afraid these may be a mite overdue."

Roberta flipped open each book and gave Helen a rueful smile. "Yes, indeedy! But not by much. You only owe ten cents."

Helen pulled out her wallet. As she paid, she noticed a toddler in a bouncy chair behind Roberta. "Is she yours?" They had the same dark curls.

Roberta glanced behind her, then smiled at Helen. "That's Wendy. My babysitter had an appointment this morning, so I had to bring her to work with me."

Helen leaned on the counter and waved at the little girl while Roberta continued to check in people's books. The line had grown quite long.

"Hi, Bob," Roberta said to the person who had just stepped up in the line.

"Hello, Roberta. Oh, we meet again, Helen."

Helen turned away from Wendy and glanced up. Bob Parr smiled down at her.

"Wow," Helen said, eyeing the enormous stack of books he was holding. "Aren't those heavy?"

Bob's brows knit in confusion, and he looked down. His eyes widened at the pile of books in his arms as if he'd never seen them before. His shoulders slumped and the books suddenly looked like they weighed a ton. "Yeah. They are," he admitted. Then he chuckled. "I guess you could say I've been doing some heavy reading."

Helen laughed. Bob dropped the books on the counter with a thud. Roberta started to check them back in.

"Who's the little angel in the bouncy chair?" Bob asked.

Wendy's face scrunched up and she let out a howl.

Roberta winced. "Not always an angel."

Bob looked stricken. "What'd I do?"

"It's not you," Roberta assured him. "She's been cranky all morning." She looked over her shoulder at the wailing little girl. "It's okay, sweetie."

Roberta sped up her check-in and checkout

procedures, stamping return dates on cards with one hand while tossing books into the return bins with the other. "I'm so sorry," she said to the long line of people waiting. "Hush, sweetie. Shhhh," she crooned over her shoulder.

Wendy kept screaming.

Helen could see that the folks waiting in line with their books weren't exactly thrilled by the screaming child. Roberta looked embarrassed and torn between picking up her daughter and taking care of the patrons.

"Wendy, oh, W-e-e-endy . . ." Helen crooned. The little girl looked at her, curious. She was still crying, but at least she wasn't shrieking anymore. Then someone dropped a book on the floor and the loud sound set her off again.

Bob stepped up beside Helen. He covered his eyes. "Wendy, look. Peekaboo! Ohhhhhhh, peekaboo!"

Still crying, the little girl's attention went to Bob. He scrunched up his nose and crossed his eyes. "Look how silly I am!"

Wendy started to calm down.

"And me!" Helen stuck out her tongue. She

gripped her ears and waggled them. "I'm silly, too!"

Bob and Helen kept making faces at Wendy until she started to giggle. By then, Roberta had checked everyone's books and the line was gone.

"Oh, thank you, you two!" she said gratefully. She turned and picked up Wendy. "Now say bye-bye to the nice people."

"You mean the silly people!" Bob made a ridiculous face at Wendy.

"The very silly people!" Helen made an even more ridiculous face.

The little girl laughed and clapped.

"Well, goodbye, silly people," Roberta said. "See you soon!"

Bob and Helen strolled to the door. Bob bowed. "After you, goofball."

Helen laughed. "Why, thank you, wack-a-doodle!"

They stepped outside. "Well, I go that way," Helen said.

"And I'm the other direction," replied Bob.

They turned away from each other. After a few steps, Helen turned around. At the exact same moment, Bob turned around, too.

Helen blushed, then stuck out her tongue.

Bob laughed and wiggled his nose.

"Bye!" they each called.

Helen started walking home. *Boy, if they only knew how funny my faces could have been....* She pictured all the ways she could have stretched her features to entertain Wendy. By the time she was home, she was laughing out loud.

Elastigirl was still chuckling about her encounter with Bob Parr when the phone rang. "Hello?" she said.

"Rick Dicker wants all Supers at NSA headquarters," said the nasal-voiced woman on the other end of the line. Elastigirl immediately recognized the voice as belonging to Shirley.

"Again? Why?" Elastigirl asked.

"Trouble afoot. Big emergency."

Elastigirl stifled a laugh. Only Shirley could sound bored when announcing an emergency. "I'll be right there."

A few minutes later, Elastigirl took the elevator to the top floor of the building that housed the National Supers Agency. At the end of the hallway just outside the conference room, Elastigirl saw a large poster board set up on an easel. *That's new,* she thought, stepping up to it.

"'This Week in Crime-Fighting,'" she read aloud. Rows of mug shots were taped to the board. The names of the criminals were written neatly under each photo, along with the name of the Super responsible for each capture. She wondered if the poster would work as incentive or create tension among the Supers. She noticed almost every single picture was of a criminal apprehended by Blazestone. "That's one Super who has been working overtime," Elastigirl observed.

"What'd you say?" Apogee asked as she came up beside Elastigirl.

"Oh, sorry, App. Just thinking out loud," Elastigirl said. "Do you have any idea what this meeting is all about?" she asked as they headed into the conference room.

"Not a clue." Apogee scanned the room. "But it must be serious if they called all of us in."

"I guess we'll find out now." Elastigirl watched Rick Dicker's progress from the door to the podium, followed by the ever-faithful Shirley, who was carrying an enormous file. Today she wore plaid trousers and a sweater decorated with embroidered butterflies. Her usually frizzy hair had been ironed flat, and the ends curled up in a little flip.

Dicker stepped up to the mike and cleared his throat. The buzz in the room hushed as the Supers gave him their attention. Elastigirl could tell everyone was curious about what Rick Dicker might have to say.

"Thank you for coming. I'll get right to it. As you know, we are conducting experiments with Zero Atomic Protocol, also known as ZAP, and its potential as a Super enhancer."

A murmur burbled among the Supers. "It seemed to help my powers stay active without daylight," Apogee commented.

"It completely messed me up!" Universal Man complained loudly.

"Did nothing for me!" Frozone called out.

"Would never touch the stuff!" Mr. Incredible added to the chorus of voices.

Elastigirl glanced over and nodded. She agreed with Mr. I.

Rick Dicker waited for the voices to die down,

then continued. "Yes, the effects are unpredictable. That's why it's considered experimental . . . and why we use small doses."

"So why are we here?" Frozone asked. "What's up?"

Rick Dicker took a moment to take off his glasses, clean them, and put them back on. "A new shipment of ZAP has disappeared."

Elastigirl heard the gasps all over the room.

Dicker held up a hand to quiet them down. "This *could* just be an administrative mix-up."

Shirley stood up straighter and glared at Dicker. Clearly she didn't like him suggesting she had made a mistake.

"But it is far more likely that it was stolen," Dicker said. "This is very concerning. In addition to questions about its effects on your powers, if it's not handled correctly, it can have explosive tendencies."

Elastigirl gasped. "And you were experimenting on Supers with it?" she demanded.

"Not cool, Dicker," Mr. Incredible said. He looked at Elastigirl. He had the same disapproving expression on his face that Elastigirl figured was on hers. They both shook their heads in disbelief. It was still unclear how the other Supers felt about it.

Dicker held up his hand. "I said it's explosive *if* it's used incorrectly. We know what we're doing. You put yourselves at risk every day on behalf of the citizens of Municiberg. The NSA would never add to that risk. We value you all, which is one of the reasons we instituted Supers Appreciation Day. To show our support and admiration publicly."

Dicker paused and eyed the group. Elastigirl did the same. Dicker's answer seemed to satisfy most of them. She noticed Mr. Incredible still looked skeptical, which was how she felt, too. Who would've guessed the two of them would be in such agreement?

Dicker cleared his throat. "But about Supers Appreciation Day. It makes the timing of this theft even more worrisome. We are concerned that an unknown Super Villain may be building a massive weapon and planning to use it while the Supers are attending the awards ceremony."

This time Dicker didn't need to quiet the room. The Supers stood in stunned silence. They shifted on their feet and cast confused and worried glances at one another.

This is just what I was afraid of, Elastigirl thought with horror. *That the bad guys would take advantage of the distraction of all the festivities.*

"I'm surprised there are any villains left to come up with a plot," Downburst called out from near the poster board. "Blazestone has caught so many."

All heads turned in Downburst's direction.

"Thanks, kid," Blazestone called back.

"Awwww," Gamma Jack teased Downburst. "How sweet."

Downburst opened and closed his mouth, and his eyes dropped to his boots.

Elastigirl smiled. Whether he'd meant to do it or not, Downburst had broken the tension. Several of the Supers chuckled. A few gave Blazestone thumbs-ups.

"Don't pay any attention to Gamma Jack," Apogee told Downburst. She patted him on the back. "We're *all* proud of the work Blazestone has been doing."

"Be that as it may," Rick Dicker continued, "we

are considering cancelling Supers Appreciation Day."

"Isn't it too late for that?" Blazestone asked.

"But—but—but—" Mr. Incredible sputtered. "The fans will be so disappointed!"

Not just the fans, Elastigirl thought. Mr. Incredible seriously wanted to be in that Supers Appreciation Day parade. As she listened to all the objections being shouted at Rick Dicker, she realized a lot more Supers were limelight-lovers than she had thought.

Elastigirl raised her hand as Supers complained and disagreed around her. But Mr. Incredible had moved in front of her, blocking Dicker's view. She stretched her arm until her hand appeared over Mr. Incredible's blond head.

"Yes, Elastigirl?" Rick Dicker said.

"I volunteer to bow out of the Supers Appreciation Day events to patrol in the rest of the city. That way the festivities can proceed as planned."

Rick Dicker nodded slowly. "Perhaps that could—"

"Me too!" Blazestone said, pushing her way to the front of the room. "I'll give up attending the ceremonies." She turned to address the whole group. "You can just have someone accept my awards for me when I win," she added with a smirk.

"Have you checked the weather report?" Universal Man said, his voice dripping with disdain.

Uh-oh. Elastigirl pursed her lips. *Universal Man must still be smarting from Blazestone's rooster comment the other day.* She worried about how Blazestone would respond to the obvious burn.

Blazestone held up her hands as if she were surrendering. "Right you are. I'll patrol as long as it's not raining. And if it is, then I'll be able to pick up those awards myself, live and in person!"

Elastigirl was impressed that the usually volatile Blazestone had taken Universal Man's insult in stride. Maybe her rough edges were starting to smooth a little. Still, Elastigirl wouldn't be surprised if Blazestone's offer to help was simply because she was eager to take down more bad guys. According to the rules Dicker had droned on and on about, the tally for the award for most criminals caught was to be done just minutes before the ceremony. Any villain Blazestone caught while out patrolling would be added to her total.

Elastigirl supposed that meant the award and the key to the city could also go to *her*, Elastigirl—if there were enough criminals to stop. She hoped there wouldn't be. An award just wasn't as important as finding that ZAP and making sure Municiberg was safe, both for Supers *and* the citizens!

"Uh . . . do you think I could . . . that is . . . can I patrol, too?" Downburst offered.

"Sure thing, kiddo." Blazestone strolled through the group and slung her arm across Downburst's shoulders. "Maybe the three of us should form our own alliance. You, me, and Elastigirl."

A big smile spread across Downburst's flushed face. Elastigirl snuck a peek at Universal Man. He stood across the room at the windows with crossed arms, silently fuming. She knew Blazestone had only said that to rile him—and it seemed to have worked.

"I'll help out." Mr. Incredible held up a hand.

"Don't forget, Mr. I," Frozone said from the

doorway, where he was leaning against the door-jamb. "We've got that appearance at the screening of our cartoon."

"Wouldn't think of missing that," Mr. Incredible assured Frozone. Then he addressed Elastigirl: "But I'll check in whenever I'm not busy with any of my scheduled Supers Appreciation Day events."

Elastigirl was surprised. She'd figured he'd want to spend all his time being *appreciated*.

"Sure," Elastigirl said. "The more the merrier. As long as you don't get in the way."

Mr. Incredible raised an eyebrow. Then he put a hand over his heart and gave a slight bow. "Wouldn't dream of it."

○ ○ ○

"You have to remember this is just a prototype," Downburst explained. "I haven't worked out all the bugs yet."

Elastigirl and Downburst were riding down the elevator in the NSA building after the meeting broke up. Downburst had been given a small lab in which to practice his atomic matter manipulation. He was going to show her his most recent attempt at making a speedier bicycle solely by rearranging atoms.

"Don't worry, I understand," Elastigirl assured him. "Everything goes through a research-and-development phase. After all, nothing—Supers included—starts out perfect."

She was fond of the shy fellow and knew how much he craved the approval of the more established and experienced Supers. She hoped she could provide some encouragement. "How did you start working on bicycles?"

"Oh." Downburst looked a little embarrassed. "I wanted to make myself a special exercise bike," he confided. He patted his slightly pudgy belly. "To get into better shape. These Supersuits show every extra pound."

"Did you succeed?" Elastigirl asked as she followed him out of the elevator.

"Not exactly," he admitted. "I—I couldn't control it. I'd try to go faster, and instead of speeding up it would spin around. And then when I tried to slow down, the pedals spun backward. But it gave me some ideas about making a bicycle that could adapt to its surroundings," he added quickly.

"That sounds promising!" Elastigirl said. "It would be great if I could have a bike that changed size and shape along with me."

"That's what I was thinking, too."

He opened the door to his lab, and Elastigirl stepped inside. She gaped at the sight of the crowded and messy room. Bits and pieces of handlebars, wheels, spokes, and other unidentifiable parts were scattered everywhere. Some had obviously burned; others looked as if they had exploded from the inside out. Still others were completely misshapen, mangled, and bent out of shape.

Downburst bustled around, tidying up. "Sorry for the mess," he said, opening a file drawer and stashing a half-eaten sandwich inside. "I wasn't expecting a visitor."

Elastigirl carefully stepped around a large pile of tools. "No problem. Where's the new model?" she asked.

"Over here." He led her to a platform at the far end of the room. An empty platform.

"Is it invisible?" Elastigirl asked with excitement. "That would be really cool!"

"No. But that's a good idea. I'll have to try

that, too." Downburst bent down and picked up something Elastigirl couldn't see. When he turned, he held out his open palm. "This is it."

Elastigirl peered at his hand. "Ohhhhhh." He was holding a tiny bicycle.

"I've been working on making the world's most portable bike. You can carry this in your pocket." He knelt down and placed the tiny bike back on the platform. "But then, just by splashing some water on it, it will grow. Like this!"

He carefully put down the miniature bike and picked up a glass of water that was sitting beside the platform. Elastigirl had assumed it was just part of Downburst's messiness, unrelated to his inventions.

Downburst took a deep breath. "Please work," he murmured softly. He sprinkled a few drops of water onto the tiny bicycle. He took a step back and gestured for Elastigirl to do the same.

For a moment nothing happened. Then there was a squeaking sound. Elastigirl's eyes widened as the tiny bike expanded. First the back wheel. Then the handlebars. The seat. Then the front wheel. The pedals.

Downbursts and Elastigirl waited. And waited. Finally, Elastigirl said, "Oh."

The bike was no longer tiny. But none of the pieces looked like they belonged on the same bike. The back wheel was huge, nearly to the ceiling. The front wheel was normal-sized. The handlebars were on backward. The pedals stuck out of the seat, which was upside down.

Downburst sighed.

Elastigirl patted his arm. "Nothing gets figured out all at once. But I think you're really onto something. You got it to go from teeny-tiny to . . . well, this."

Downburst sighed again. "A completely useless thing."

"It's a big accomplishment," Elastigirl insisted. "You made something out of nothing. And then made that something change. That's the very definition of atomic manipulation!"

"You think?"

Elastigirl nodded. "You just need to keep working on it."

"Thanks, Elastigirl." He gave her a big smile. "I know you always turn down the offers to become a team leader. But I think you'd make a really good one."

"Nah," Elastigirl said. "It's hard to be part of a team, much less lead one. I don't think I'm cut out for it."

"I want to be on a team someday," Downburst told her. "That's my biggest aspiration."

"Keep working on your skills," Elastigirl said. "I'm sure the NSA will assign you one of these days."

"I hope so," Downburst said. He stepped onto the platform and maneuvered the misshapen bike to the side. He leaned it against the wall, since the kickstand was woven through the spokes of the back wheel. "Maybe even with Blazestone. I don't think she's very happy with Universal Man."

"I think you're right about that."

He turned and cocked his head as he studied Elastigirl. "I guess you and she are kind of alike."

"Really? How do you figure?" Elastigirl asked. This was the second time she'd been compared to Blazestone. First time was by Frozone, who knew her really well. And now by a Super she was just getting to know.

"Neither one of you is all that into teams," Downburst explained.

Elastigirl frowned. *Am I like Blazestone? Nah,* she told herself. Blazestone was really impulsive; she could be downright reckless at times. *And boy, does that Super like to boast.* Still... Elastigirl wondered if she was being too harsh. She and Blazestone *did* prefer doing things their own way. They wanted to get through the red tape and just cut to the chase. They were ready at all times for whatever might be thrown their way. And they both were less than enthusiastic about Supers Appreciation Day. Maybe Downburst had a point.

"I'll have to give that some thought," she told him. "And you"—she pointed at him and waggled her finger—"you keep working on these bicycles. I'm looking for some Super transport and I think you're my best bet."

"Really? Wow." Downburst jumped off the platform and began rummaging through his pile of tools. "You got it, Elastigirl! I'll come up with something perfect just for you."

CHAPTER 11

The next morning, Elastigirl rolled out of bed and turned on the radio. Then she went into the bathroom to brush her teeth.

"We certainly couldn't have picked a better day for our very first Municiberg Supers Appreciation Day," the radio announcer declared. "Blue skies, perfect temperature."

"That'll be good for Blazestone," Elastigirl said to her reflection in the mirror.

She slipped on her Supersuit and headed out. She was going to meet Blazestone and Downburst at NSA headquarters for a last-minute briefing.

As Elastigirl strolled through the bustling streets, people waved and cheered at her.

"Look, Elastigirl!" a little girl wearing a white leotard and a homemade cardboard mask shouted. "I'm you!"

"Great costume!" Elastigirl gave the young fan a thumbs-up.

All around her she saw costumed citizens, large and small, smiling and admiring each other's outfits. Fans carrying signs declaring their love for various Supers planted themselves along the parade route. The whole city had a festive feeling. Elastigirl just hoped there wouldn't be any trouble. It would be a shame if anything put a damper on the great spirit of excitement all around her. She noticed even *she* had a skip in her step as she entered the NSA headquarters. Feeling all that genuine affection from the fans—not just for her but for all the Supers—made her feel, well, *appreciated*, just like the event promised. And she had to admit, it wasn't half bad.

Blazestone had already arrived and stood in the hallway outside the conference room. She was studying the poster with the photos of all the criminals caught in the past week. She had apprehended most of them.

"Admiring your work?" Elastigirl asked as she strolled up to the other Super.

Blazestone laughed. "And yours." She pointed to the pictures of Mysterious Melvin and the electronics thieves on the board.

Rick Dicker stepped out of his office. Shirley waddled behind him, carrying a clipboard. Elastigirl couldn't help staring. Shirley was wearing a ratty old housedress. At work.

Shirley noticed Elastigirl gaping at her. "I was in the middle of getting dressed for the ceremonies," she snapped. "Then I was called in to this surprise meeting."

Dicker gestured for them to follow him into the conference room.

Blazestone and Elastigirl filed in behind him. He took his usual place at the podium. Shirley stood by his side. Elastigirl and Blazestone exchanged amused looks. It wasn't like Dicker was going to need a microphone to address just the two of them, but he was going to use it anyway, out of habit.

Dicker looked first at Blazestone and then at Elastigirl and frowned. He held out his hand.

Shirley put the clipboard into it. Dicker flipped through the pages and asked, "Weren't there three of you scheduled? You two and that new one. Downer. Downhill. Down—"

"Downburst here and reporting for duty!" Downburst raced into the conference room, red-faced and breathing hard. "Sorry I'm late," he huffed as he jogged up to the podium.

"Harrumph." Dicker rubbed his eyes.

"I had to deliver a prototype bike to the band shell," Downburst explained. "There's going to be a demonstration later." He leaned close to Elastigirl. "I think I've come up with something you're gonna love."

"Can't wait!" Elastigirl told him. She squeezed his arm.

Dicker consulted the clipboard again. "Oh, yes. You've been working on the two-wheeled mutable transportation systems."

"Also known as bicycles?" Blazestone asked with a grin.

"*Mutable* bicycles," Dicker corrected.

"They can change form," Downburst explained

earnestly. Elastigirl was pleased by the pride he seemed to be taking in his work.

"Uh, yeah, I figured that out," Blazestone said, smirking.

"Oh." Confusion, then embarrassment, flickered across Downburst's face. "Sorry. I didn't mean . . ."

And there goes all that self-confidence, Elastigirl observed. She'd have to have a little talk with Blazestone about Downburst. He obviously had a huge crush on the Super. Elastigirl was sure Blazestone didn't *mean* to be mean. Well, pretty sure. Well, she hoped she didn't, at least.

"Anyway, I have a few more pieces of equipment that may be useful in the current circumstances," Dicker told them. He waggled his fingers, and Shirley hoisted a large box onto the podium. Dicker pulled out a belt. It had a walkie-talkie resting in a holster dangling from it. "You will use these radios to contact each other or to call in to the NSA if you need backup or have a criminal we should bring in."

Shirley pulled the belts from the box and gave

one to each of the Supers. Elastigirl buckled hers around her waist. She was a bit concerned about what would happen to it if she needed to stretch. From what she could see, it wasn't made out of a special stretchable material like her Supersuit. She supposed she'd figure it out if and when that time came.

"I also want you to add a Super locator to your crime alert signals." Dicker held up something that looked like a compass. "That way you can find each other quickly if you get separated. You can also use it if for some reason you are unable to speak into the radios."

Once again, Shirley dug into the box, then handed the locators around.

Turning it over, Elastigirl saw that the Super locator had a clip on the back. She slipped it onto her headband next to her crime alert button.

"And lastly," Rick Dicker said, "we came up with devices that will detect the presence of ZAP. These should prove invaluable."

He picked up a small box. Elastigirl eyed it dubiously. "Uh, sir," she said, "how are we supposed to apprehend criminals carrying those things around?"

Dicker turned the box in all directions, studying it from each angle. "Hmmm. The designers did seem to forget how active you need to be. They were intended for inspectors, not Supers."

"I might be able to come up with something," Downburst offered.

Dicker raised an eyebrow, uncertain. Then he sighed. "Go for it," he said—not very enthusiastically, Elastigirl noticed.

Downburst stepped forward. He twisted his mouth, thinking, then scratched his head. Snapping his fingers, he turned to Dicker. "Can I borrow your tie, sir?"

Dicker looked surprised, shrugged, and then pulled off his tie and handed it to Downburst. Elastigirl was curious. What was Downburst going to do?

While Downburst laid the borrowed tie across the podium, Dicker and Shirley exchanged a look. Then they ducked out the door.

"Uh, should we be worried?" Blazestone asked.

"I'm narrowing my focus to just a very small area," Downburst assured her, lining up the three ZAP detectors behind the podium. "You should be fine."

"'Should be,'" Blazestone muttered. "Doesn't exactly fill me with confidence."

"Don't distract him," Elastigirl whispered.

Concentrating hard, Downburst reached out his hands. For a moment, nothing happened. Then the tie wiggled like an angry snake and, suddenly, split into several pieces.

"Do you think that's what was supposed to happen?" Blazestone whispered.

"Shhh," Elastigirl whispered back. She wasn't sure, either.

"Not exactly *borrowed*, was it?" Dicker muttered, poking his head back into the room. "That's one tie I'll never see again."

Next the ZAP detectors began vibrating on the podium. They shimmered, shook, and rumbled. Then—*poof!* There was a flash of light, and the bits of Dicker's tie had become pairs of straps attached to the sides of each of the boxes.

"Wow!" Elastigirl gasped. "Well done."

"See! Now we can wear the boxes like backpacks!" Downburst announced proudly. He stepped up to the podium and picked up a ZAP detector. "Hm."

"Something wrong?" Dicker asked. "Did you destroy the detectors? Those are very expensive!"

"No, the box is fine," Downburst said hastily. "It's the straps. They're a little . . . small."

He tried slinging a strap over one shoulder, but it didn't even go all the way up his arm.

Elastigirl hated his look of disappointment. "I have an idea!" She took the box from Downburst. "We'll attach them to our radio belts. So we'll still be hands-free!"

Downburst looked relieved. "Actually, that's an even better idea. We wouldn't be able to see the readings if we were wearing them on our backs."

Elastigirl, Blazestone, and Downburst slid their belts through the straps of the detectors. Elastigirl felt a bit weighed down by the extra devices, but the precautions were probably worth it. They had no idea what—or who—they were going up against. Better to be over-prepared than under.

Dicker checked his wristwatch. "You should get going. The parade has already started. That means most Supers are otherwise engaged and the city will be vulnerable."

Downburst snapped to attention and gave Dicker a sharp salute. "We're on it, sir!"

Dicker blinked. Shirley stared.

Elastigirl raised her hand and saluted, too. She didn't want Downburst to feel bad. He was already thrown by the straps mishap. "We sure are," she said.

Blazestone looked quizzically at Elastigirl, then shrugged. She gave a half-hearted salute. "Yeah, what they said."

"Report anything suspicious," Dicker said. "Stay alert out there."

"Always do!" Elastigirl said.

The three Supers turned and headed for the elevators.

"One last thing," Dicker called after them. The three Supers stopped and turned. "Anyone you apprehend, bring to NSA for questioning, no matter how minor the infraction. The timing is just too worrisome. We don't want to take any chances that someone armed with ZAP is out there being a danger."

"Understood," Elastigirl told him. She, Blazestone, and Downburst continued to the elevator.

"I saw Mr. Incredible when I dropped off the bike at the band shell," Downburst told them, punching the elevator call button. "He said he'll meet up with us after the screening."

"What screening?" Blazestone asked.

"The one Mr. Incredible is over the moon about," Elastigirl laughed. She now remembered that Blazestone's attention had been elsewhere during that part of the meeting.

"Oh, right . . . that," Blazestone said.

"It's going to be a Saturday morning cartoon series," Downburst said as the elevator doors opened with a *ding*. They stepped inside, and Elastigirl pressed the button for the lobby. "The premiere's at town hall right before the parade."

"'Mr. Incredible and *Friends*'?" Blazestone said. "Who else is in it?"

Downburst shrugged. "I don't know."

"Frozone for one, I bet," Elastigirl said. "They're really close."

"That would be 'and *friend*,' not *friends*," Blazestone said. "I wonder if they're going to want me for the series."

"I'm sure they will," Downburst told her. "You're awesome."

Blazestone flicked her ponytail and chucked him under the chin. "Thanks, kid."

The elevator doors opened into the lobby and the Supers whirled through the revolving door onto the sidewalk.

"Where should we start?" Downburst asked when they were outside. He tossed his cape over his shoulder and planted his hands on his hips just above his belt. "I'm ready to keep Municiberg safe!"

"About that," Blazestone said. "I'm thinking we should split up."

"But I thought we were a team," Downburst said, deflating a little.

"We can cover more territory if we go our separate ways," Blazestone said.

"She has a point," Elastigirl said. "We'll stay in touch, but we kinda want eyes everywhere. And that's not going to happen if we're together."

"I guess you're right," Downburst said reluctantly.

Elastigirl knew he was disappointed, but she agreed with Blazestone. They really did need to cover as much ground as possible.

"I'm going to do an aerial reconnaissance to start," Blazestone said. Using her ability to ride warm air currents, she leapt into the air and propelled herself above the tree line. "See you later!" She whooshed away.

Elastigirl watched her fly off, then turned to Downburst. She and Downburst were going to be doing their patrolling on foot. "I go left, you go right?" she suggested.

"Sure thing."

Elastigirl turned and started marching through the streets, senses on high alert. Sure, Dicker had said it was possible the missing shipment wasn't really missing. Just a clerical error. But she didn't believe it, and she was sure Dicker didn't, either. If the ZAP wound up in the wrong hands, there could be a world of trouble. It was still unclear what effect the radioactive stuff had—and that could spell disaster.

So was it stolen as a way to neutralize Supers, Elastigirl wondered, *or was the criminal interested in the ZAP for some other nefarious purpose?* A device to terrify the citizens of Municiberg? To use to get into a bank vault? There were so many possibilities. All of them bad.

She heard cheers coming from the other side of the office buildings. She was moving parallel to the parade route. She stretched herself so she could see over the rooftops. Her NSA-issued belt swiveled around her hips but stayed put. Good. It passed the stretch test.

The parade of Supers marched along the street, waving at fans. Frozone created snowballs and tossed them to gleeful kids. Flying Supers gave giddy children airborne rides. Gamma Jack blew kisses, making more than one female fan swoon.

Seeing all the excited people, some in costumes, others carrying signs, all smiling, Elastigirl was even more determined to protect them and Municiberg. She was starting to understand Mr. Incredible's enthusiasm for the event. Maybe he really had meant it when he'd claimed he wanted the parade stops and photo ops "for the fans" and not his own ego. These folks seemed thrilled any time a Super made personal contact—a handshake, an autograph, or even just a smile and a wave.

A sudden movement brought her attention back down to the ground. Her head whipped around. What was it? The street she stood on was empty. Everyone was enjoying the parade.

Bingo! From her vantage point with her head high above the ground, Elastigirl spotted someone hunched over and sneaking along the row of parked cars three blocks away. *If that doesn't look suspicious, I don't know what would.* Elastigirl crossed the distance in just two steps. The person was slipping a wire into the door of a red car, obviously trying to break in. Elastigirl reached down and hoisted the would-be car thief high into the air.

"I don't think so," she declared as he kicked and squirmed.

The guy stopped struggling and became dead weight in her hands. "What do you know about the ZAP?" she asked him as she strode back to NSA headquarters.

"The what?"

"ZAP," Elastigirl repeated. "ZAP."

The criminal laughed. "Like a bug zapper?"

"Oh, shush," Elastigirl snapped. She'd leave it to Rick Dicker to interrogate this criminal. She started to reach for her radio but found there was a flaw in their communication system. Now that she was super-stretched, the radio on her belt was far below her. On top of that, she'd need to release one of her hands holding the bad guy to press the button on the radio. No matter. She hadn't gotten very far from headquarters. She'd just drop this guy off with Dicker for a cross-examination and then get back out on patrol.

She quickly strode through the streets.

"Wow. This is some view," the would-be car thief commented, his head swiveling around. "Hey! I can see my apartment from up here."

"Oh, be quiet," Elastigirl said. "This isn't a sightseeing tour."

She shrank back down to regular size to get into the building. Keeping a tight grip on the guy with her hands, she picked up the phone on the reception desk with her foot.

"Dicker? I've got one for you."

She hung up and studied her catch. "What's your name?" she asked. She was trying to place him. He looked familiar.

"What's it to ya?" the man snarled.

The elevator doors slid open and an NSA security detail piled out. One of them frowned. "He doesn't look so dangerous."

"Hey!" the man protested. "I'm notorious."

"Dicker said to bring any and all criminals in for NSA interrogation," Elastigirl explained. "I don't think he's involved with the ZAP theft," she added. "But he *was* trying to steal a car." Then she remembered her ZAP detector. "Hang on." She lifted the box and held it toward the car thief. Nothing. "Okay, he's clear," she said.

"Then we'll take it from here," the head security guy said.

"Why does he look so familiar?" Elastigirl asked. "Is there an APB out on him or something?"

The security guard studied the criminal.

"Got a good look?" the criminal sneered. "Take a picture, it'll last longer."

Elastigirl snapped her fingers. "Picture! Of

course! He's one of the criminals Blazestone brought in this week. His picture is up on the board." She stepped up to the guy. "How'd you get away?"

"Wouldn't you like to know?" he retorted.

"It's rare, but jailbreaks sometimes happen," the security man admitted. "Come on, you." He nudged the prisoner toward the elevator.

Elastigirl marched back outside. The sounds of the parade were much fainter. She decided to stay in this part of town. After all, there were lots of Supers and police around the parade route. If a villain wanted to take advantage of the distraction created by the special events, it would probably happen away from all the activities.

Once again, she stretched her legs to cover more ground. She quickly found herself in an unfamiliar area. She lengthened her neck to get her bearings.

Then she spotted someone in a hazmat suit... wearing a pair of oversized thick gloves. Just the kind of attire a person might need if they were going to handle radioactive materials! *Stolen* radioactive materials.

Go slow, she told herself. She didn't want to spook him. She needed to first determine whether or not he had the ZAP on him. There was no telling what he might do with it if he felt cornered. And she had no idea what would happen to her or her powers if she came into contact with it.

She brought herself back to her regular size, keeping him in sight, but staying far enough away that he wouldn't notice her. The streets were deserted; otherwise people would have stopped to stare at his bizarre outfit. The criminal had probably planned it this way, timing things to get through the area undetected. Elastigirl was relieved. No one would get hurt if it came down to a battle between them.

When he rounded a corner, she counted to five, then stretched her neck around the corner to watch where he was going. She saw a familiar group of trees. *Now* she knew where she was. The back entrance to the zoo was just a few blocks away. Could he be planning to use the ZAP on the animals? Create radioactive lions and tigers?

She wasn't going to let that happen!

With just a few well-executed gymnastic flips

and somersaults, she landed right behind him. She knocked him to the ground and yanked off the helmet part of the hazmat suit.

Her jaw dropped when she realized who it was.

The zookeeper? Behind the radioactive heist?

She couldn't believe it!

Unbelievable, maybe, but true. He was going to turn the animals into radioactive beasts! What a horrible plot.

"Why?" Elastigirl asked. "Why would you do this?"

"I didn't have a choice," the zookeeper explained. "The woman who takes care of the bees has the flu. Believe me, I didn't want to. But I have to go check on them."

"What?" That didn't sound right. She quickly slid the ZAP detector into position. Nothing. This just didn't make any sense. "Bees?"

The zookeeper shuddered. "I hate bees. And Missy's beekeeping outfit was way too small for me. This was the best I could do for bee protection. I hope it does the trick."

Ooops. "Sorry about knocking you over," Elastigirl said. She helped him back to his feet.

"The hazmat suit . . . I, uh, I thought you were someone else."

"Oh, that's okay," the zookeeper said amiably. "It's not like I'm in a hurry to face those stingers!"

"Well, again—apologies. Go about your work. And don't get stung."

"Thanks for your concern, Elastigirl," he said. "Maybe I'll see you later at the awards ceremony."

She watched as he trundled toward the zoo.

So far she had caught one criminal with no obvious link to the ZAP theft and pounced on an innocent bystander. She hoped the rest of the day would be more productive.

She was debating which way to go when she heard someone call her name. She turned to see Downburst.

"How's it going?" she asked as Downburst jogged toward her.

"Really quiet out there," he reported. "Haven't seen anything suspicious."

Blazestone came around the opposite corner. She startled when she saw them, then laughed. "How'd we all wind up in the same place?"

"Have you found anything to help us locate the

ZAP or whoever took it?" Elastigirl asked.

Blazestone shook her head, making her ponytail bounce. "Nope. You?"

"Not us, either," Downburst said. He scratched his chin. "Maybe the NSA was wrong. Maybe there isn't any terrible plot afoot."

"Could be," Blazestone said.

"A weird thing happened, though," Elastigirl said. "I apprehended a car thief—"

"Good for you!" Blazestone said.

"But here's the thing," Elastigirl continued. "*You* had already caught him. Last week."

Blazestone looked shocked. "Are you sure?" she asked.

"The guard confirmed it," Elastigirl said.

"Wow. That *is* weird."

"Maybe somehow he used the ZAP to escape," Downburst suggested.

"I didn't think of that," Elastigirl admitted. "Though he didn't seem like he knew anything about it. And he didn't register on the ZAP detector."

Blazestone fiddled with the ZAP box dangling from her belt. "Could be the boxes don't work," she suggested.

"Or they only work if there's enough ZAP to set it off," Elastigirl said. "We never did a field test. So it's hard to know."

"I hope the ZAP will enhance my powers," Downburst said. "Like it does for Apogee."

"I think that stuff is way too risky to play around with," Blazestone said. "I can't believe Apogee would want to experiment with it."

"She did seem really keen on it," Downburst mused. "Before it got stolen, she was telling me all about how transformative ZAP could be."

Blazestone and Elastigirl shared a worried look. "Do you think . . . ?" Blazestone began.

Downburst's jaw dropped. "You think Apogee . . . ?"

"She did seem to like the ZAP a lot more than anyone else," Blazestone said. "And it would help remove the limits on her powers. . . ."

"Let's not jump to conclusions," Elastigirl said. "Apogee would never betray us." *Would she . . . ?* "Let's get back to patrolling."

After deciding who would go where, the Supers separated again.

Elastigirl frowned as she strode away from the

zoo area. She didn't like thinking that Apogee was a traitor to the NSA and the other Supers. She kicked a pebble in the street and it sailed out of sight. A moment later, she heard the sound of tinkling glass. "Hey!" someone exclaimed in the distance. *Oooops.* Sometimes she forgot she had strength in addition to stretch. She'd make sure to fix what she had broken later.

"Don't jump to conclusions," Elastigirl told herself. "But don't let your friendship blind you, either. Think carefully."

Elastigirl thought back to her conversations with Apogee about ZAP. She had been pretty excited about it. And Elastigirl had never gotten the story about why Apogee's team, the Thrilling Three, had disbanded. Could it be Apogee harbored some resentment toward Supers or the NSA?

Elastigirl was still mulling over the evidence when Downburst's voice crackled over her radio, interrupting her train of thought. "Blazestone! Elastigirl! I could use some backup!"

"On my way," Elastigirl responded. She found him on her locator. He wasn't very far away. It looked like the quickest way to get there would be off the ground. She reached up and grabbed the ladder of the fire escape attached to the building that rose above her. She quickly clambered up, then flipped and somersaulted from building roof to building roof. She spotted Downburst below, chasing someone who looked like—Elastigirl?!

Elastigirl couldn't believe what she was seeing. The red boots. The E on the front. Even the red headband! *Who stole my signature style?*

Downburst wasn't as fast as the villain. She was getting away.

Elastigirl leapt to the ground. "I'm here, Downburst," she called. She was beside him in two steps of her stretched legs.

"I'm going to try to wall her in," Downburst said.

He flung out his hands. They emitted some kind of ray that looked like ripples in the air. The sidewalks shimmered, and the curb wiggled and grew. . . .

Two inches.

But it was enough to trip the baddie. She fell over the tiny wall and landed facedown in the street. This gave Elastigirl time to stretch out her arms. She clamped her hands on the imposter and flipped her over. Then she snapped the rest of her stretched body forward to meet her hands. She retracted to her regular size as Downburst huffed up beside them.

"I detected radioactive material in her gloves," Downburst explained, his breath coming in bursts. "That's how I knew that she wasn't just a fan attending Supers Appreciation Day."

"Good work," Elastigirl said, keeping a foot planted on the squirming imposter, who still lay in the street. Her Elastigirl costume was pretty good, but she had spiky dark hair, not red. And instead of boots, she wore high-top sneakers.

"I don't know which bugs me more," Elastigirl complained, yanking the villain to her feet. "That you are involved in a terrible scheme, or that you would disguise yourself as me to do it!"

"Tell us the plan," Downburst said, dropping onto the little wall he'd made.

The villain laughed. "Wouldn't you like to know?"

"Why, yes, I would," Downburst said sincerely. "That's why I asked."

Elastigirl flipped the red cardboard mask up to the top of the villain's head. Then she took a surprised step back. "You—your picture was on the board at NSA headquarters!"

"Yeah? I hope they got my best angle. Was I having a good hair day?"

Ignoring the villain's questions, Elastigirl turned to Downburst. "Blazestone neutralized this one, too."

Downburst's eyes widened. "Someone must be helping them escape!"

Elastigirl gripped the lanyard the woman wore around her neck and pulled her close. Nose-to-nose, she snarled, "Who's your accomplice?"

The woman jerked herself backward. When she did, the laminated card dangling from the lanyard flipped over. Elastigirl grabbed it.

"'All-Access Pass,'" she read aloud. She glanced up at Downburst. "Do you know what this means?"

"That she's a VIP?"

"It means the bad guys aren't planning a crime spree while all the Supers are at the awards ceremony," Elastigirl said slowly as the plot became clear to her. "They're going to go after the Supers *at* the awards ceremony!"

The Elastigirl imposter laughed. "Brilliant idea, don't you think?"

"We've got to get over there," Elastigirl declared, her mind whirling. Her eyes flicked to the Elastigirl imposter. "Downburst, make some kind of enclosure to hold her till the NSA can pick her up. We have to get to the band shell, pronto!"

Downburst narrowed his eyes, concentrating. Stronger rays burst from his fingers. Slowly, the sidewalks burbled and rose to form a lumpy box around the criminal, trapping her inside.

"Hey!" She pounded on the walls. "Let me out! I'm going to run out of air!"

"There are plenty of airholes. But my friend can close them up if you'd prefer," Elastigirl snapped.

The villain quieted down.

"I'll tell Dicker what's going on." Elastigirl pressed a button on her radio.

"NSA here," a voice answered.

"Criminal apprehended and needs retrieval," Elastigirl said into the radio. "And we—"

Suddenly, a call broke in on the line, cutting off Elastigirl's connection to the NSA.

Blazestone's voice crackled over the radio. "I need you both now!" She sounded frantic. "At the wharf! The old fishing warehouse."

Elastigirl released her radio and grabbed Downburst's hand. "We'll call Dicker once we help Blazestone. Come on!"

"I hope she's okay," Downburst said worriedly as they ran.

As they hurried to the fishing warehouse, Elastigirl came up with a plan. "Once we help Blazestone, we'll head for the band shell. I have a feeling the situation will require all three of us."

"Do you think Apogee is behind it all?" Downburst asked when they reached the pier where the fishing warehouse stood—the same abandoned warehouse where she had nabbed the electronics thieves a week earlier. It sat on the opposite end of the wharf from the band shell, where the awards ceremony would be taking place. And possibly a battle.

Elastigirl gestured for Downburst to stay quiet. She stretched her neck to check inside. But the windows were so covered with grime and cobwebs she couldn't see anything. They'd have to go in.

Elastigirl brought her head back down. "Be ready for anything," she whispered to Downburst. He nodded, but she could see a glimmer of fear in his eyes.

Together they crept along the side of the enormous warehouse. Elastigirl held out an arm, stopping Downburst. She stretched her neck to peer around the corner of the building. This time the double metal doors stood open, the cavernous interior dark. She didn't hear anything. She hoped Blazestone was okay—that they weren't too late to bail her out of a bad situation.

Leaving her head where it was, she flicked her hand a few times. A moment later, Downburst stood beside her. She returned to her regular size and padded quietly into the silent warehouse with Downburst right behind her.

She scanned the familiar location. The stolen equipment had been confiscated by the NSA after she'd stopped the electronics heist. Now all that remained seemed to be the dusty old fishing equipment. Nets hung from the ceiling and on the walls. Rolled netting stood in barrels, like carpets waiting to be unfurled. One wall was covered with duck decoys, another with fishing rods. Steel shelving units stood in rows, filled with supplies of all kinds.

Elastigirl tipped her head. Downburst nodded. She went along one row and he went down the one next to her. They met at the end of the row and looked at each other quizzically.

"This is odd," Elastigirl said softly.

"Yeah," Downburst agreed. "No Blazestone."

"And no villains, either."

Hmmmm. Elastigirl frowned as she started putting the pieces together.

Blazestone's criminals were out and about again. Supers were going to be attacked. Blazestone, who *never* wanted help apprehending criminals, had called *both* of them as backup. A disturbing suspicion rose in Elastigirl's mind. "I don't think it's Apogee," she said.

"Then who do you think it is?" Downburst asked. "And do you think they have Blazestone?"

Elastigirl didn't want to say anything until she was sure. "Blazestone," she said into her radio. "Come in, Blazestone." No response.

"Oooo-kay..." She pulled her Super locator off her headband and punched a button. She stared down at the flashing map. "Wait, this means she's—"

"Right behind you," Downburst said.

"Hey," Blazestone snarled. "I was going to say that. Don't steal my lines!"

Elastigirl whirled around. Blazestone shot out a pyrotechnic blast. "Aaaggghhh!" Elastigirl shrieked, her hands flying to her face, trying to protect her eyes.

"No!" Downburst yelped. "I can't see!"

Blinded, Elastigirl stumbled as she stretched out her arms, desperately trying to grab Blazestone. Her hands collided with something that made a loud crash as she knocked it over. She heard another crash behind her that she assumed was Downburst trying to do the same thing.

Blinking rapidly, she was relieved when her sight began to clear. Immediately, she saw that Blazestone had vanished. Elastigirl smacked a large shipping crate in frustration.

"Where'd she go?" Downburst said, his head whipping around. "I can't believe she did that!"

"Come on," Elastigirl said. "We have to hurry. She had a head start!"

"Headquarters! Headquarters!" Downburst yelled into his radio as they ran to the enormous double doors. He glared at his radio. "Blazestone's blast shorted out our signals!" he cried.

"Whoa!" Elastigirl came to a sudden stop and threw out her arms to keep Downburst from running at the now-shut doors. "Feel that heat?"

"Blazestone must have blasted them," Downburst surmised.

They couldn't risk grabbing the handles. The doors radiated so much heat Elastigirl thought she might get singed, and those metal handles would have to be even hotter. Then she realized there was no point even *trying* to open the doors; Blazestone's heat blasts had fused the doors permanently shut.

To add insult to injury, Elastigirl could hear Blazestone chortling outside.

"But why, Blazestone?" Elastigirl called out.

"Why not?" Blazestone said with a laugh.

"That can't be it. That's not a reason," Elastigirl said.

"Fine. Here's the reason: once I get rid of the Supers, who can stop me?" Blazestone said. "I can do whatever I want, whenever I want. Rule Municiberg if I want. Or somewhere bigger and better!"

Elastigirl knew Blazestone was right. Regular law enforcement would be no match for Blazestone.

"And besides, don't all those stupid rules and regulations annoy you?" Blazestone yelled. "Sheesh! All those meetings! The forms we have to fill out in triplicate. It's enough to drive a Super right up the wall."

"Maybe so," Elastigirl conceded. "But that's still no reason to—"

"Come on! You wish you could handle things your own way, instead of by the book. Am I right?"

Elastigirl paused a moment before answering. "Sure," she admitted, "but that doesn't mean that I—"

"Oh, who cares?" Blazestone snapped. "Honestly, I've got better skills, I'm more talented, and

I'm just a whole lot more interesting than any of you silly sheep."

"We're not sheep!" Downburst shouted.

Blazestone ignored him and just kept talking. "I was a little worried when Dicker threatened to cancel the awards ceremony. That would have seriously messed with my plans. But then you, Elastigirl, solved the problem for me by volunteering to patrol."

"Glad to be of service," Elastigirl said, her mind whirling as she tried to formulate a way out.

"Yep!" Blazestone continued. "That way I could volunteer, too, giving me the perfect opportunity to put my plan into action. Speaking of which, I better fly. The best part is just moments away. This is one celebrity appearance no one will ever forget! Ta-ta!"

Elastigirl fumed. *Blazestone is so full of herself,* she thought. *And that's going to be her downfall: underestimating everyone else!*

"I can't believe I ever liked her!" Downburst said.

"We've got to get out of here. Pronto," Elastigirl said.

"I'll see if I can do anything with the doors," Downburst offered. He flung his hands out, energy sparking. The doors shimmered, and the handles elongated. "Hmmm . . ."

While Downburst kept trying to manipulate the atoms in the doors, Elastigirl scanned the warehouse. She wasn't sure how the nets and fishing rods would help them escape.

Then she realized it wasn't as dark at the opposite end of the room. She hurried through the enormous building and discovered sunlight streaming through a skylight.

"Back here!" she shouted. "We can get out this way!"

Using her power, she stretched herself up to the ceiling. "Watch out below!" she called, then smashed the glass in the skylight. Broken shards fell as Downburst skidded to a stop below her. A cool breeze blew in through the hole Elastigirl had made in the skylight.

Elastigirl stretched her hands down and lifted Downburst to the opening. He scrambled out onto the roof, and then Elastigirl hoisted herself up and through.

"It looks like the parade is still going on," Downburst reported. From their vantage point on the roof, they could see down along the wharf to the band shell on the far pier.

"That means not all the Supers are there yet," Elastigirl said. "We may still have time to stop her!"

Elastigirl lowered Downburst to the ground, then somersaulted off the roof, landing on her feet. As she brought herself back to her regular size, she brushed her hair out of her face and rearranged her headband.

"Hey, you cut yourself," Downburst said, pointing at her hands.

Elastigirl glanced at her hands. He was right. They were both bleeding. "I must have cut them when I broke the skylight."

"Let me see—"

"We have to get to the band shell," Elastigirl said. "We don't have time."

"Do you really want to run while you're bleeding?" Downburst said. "Gimme." He grabbed one of her injured hands and very carefully passed his own hand across it. Elastigirl watched, fascinated, as her skin healed itself.

He released her hand. She immediately placed her other hand in his. He healed that one, too.

"Wow, thanks," Elastigirl said. "That is one amazing power."

Downburst shrugged. "I guess."

She placed one hand on his shoulder and gazed into his eyes. "Don't 'guess,'" she instructed. "*Know.*"

Downburst nodded. "Now I know we're ready for some serious crime-fighting!"

Elastigirl adjusted her belt. "You got that right. We've got a lot of Supers to save and one hotheaded Super to stop!"

CHAPTER 12

Elastigirl and Downburst raced back to Main Street. "You keep trying to reach NSA headquarters," Elastigirl told Downburst. "Tell them what's going on, then come meet me. I'll get there faster on my own."

She stretched her legs to their full length until she towered over the warehouse. Down below, she watched a car careen around the corner. It screeched to a stop in front of Downburst. Mr. Incredible stepped out of the car. She had forgotten he was planning to patrol after the screening of his cartoon.

"Go back to the band shell!" she shouted down at Mr. Incredible.

He shielded his eyes with a hand as he gazed

up at her. “Look,” he began, sounding insulted, “I know you prefer to work alone, but–”

Elastigirl cut him off. “No! That’s where it’s all going down!” she exclaimed. “There’s going to be an attack on the Supers there!”

“Well, in that case, get in!” He hopped back inside his car. The passenger doors popped open as he leaned out the driver’s side window. “We’ll get there faster in the Incredibile!”

He was right. Elastigirl shrank back to normal size. She slid into the passenger seat beside Mr. Incredible. Downburst scrambled into the back just as Mr. Incredible started up the car.

They zoomed through town, Elastigirl and Downburst filling Mr. Incredible in on what they knew. Downburst tried his radio again. “No use,” he growled.

“Any of the gadgets in this car give you a way to communicate with the NSA?” Elastigirl asked, staring at the complicated dashboard.

“Hold down the green button,” Mr. Incredible said, his eyes on the road. The brakes squealed as he took a sharp corner and then made another high-speed turn.

Downburst leaned over the seat and reached between Mr. Incredible and Elastigirl. He pressed his thumb on the green button.

"Mayday! Mayday!" he shouted. "SOS!"

A voice came through the radio speakers. "Report, please?" the voice asked calmly.

Elastigirl slid against the passenger door as Mr. Incredible made another hair-raising turn.

"It's Blazestone!" Downburst exclaimed. "She's the one who took the ZAP! She's heading for the band shell to—"

"We know," the voice said grimly as the band shell came into view through the Incredibile's windshield.

"We're too late!" Downburst exclaimed.

Elastigirl's heart sank. Mayhem had broken out. Costumed contestants ran screaming through the streets away from the pier.

Worst of all, a giant net covered the band shell, trapping the Supers inside. *Blazestone must have taken it from the warehouse before trapping us there,* Elastigirl realized.

Chaos reigned among the Supers as they argued about the best way to escape. Mini-explosions that mixed with a terrible smell of burning rubber, electrical buzzing, and flashes of light inside the netted band shell sent citizens shrieking away, banging into each other and falling. The police tried to shepherd them to safety, but the area was packed and everyone was panicking. Some Supers were being thrown around as the radioactive materials repelled them away from the net.

Blazestone stood surrounded by helpers, most of them costumed as Supers. Any officer who approached was blasted by one of her potentially deadly rays. Two of her henchmen were dragging the mayor to a nearby tree, where Rick Dicker and Shirley were already tied up. Shirley yelled at them so loudly and persistently that one of the henchmen gagged her.

Downburst, Mr. Incredible, and Elastigirl leapt out of the Incredibile. Downburst immediately started for the band shell. Elastigirl stretched her arm and gripped his cape. She yanked him back. "We need a plan first," she told him. She glanced up at Mr. Incredible. He nodded.

"Stay away from the netting!" someone shouted from the band shell. "It's messing with our powers!"

"Let me at it!" Apogee elbowed her way through the trapped Supers. "It *enhances* my powers. I'll tear a hole for us to escape through." She flung her hands toward the netting, a fiery blast bursting out of her.

"Duck!" Elastigirl shouted. She threw herself to the ground, flattening herself to an inch thick. Mr. Incredible crouched beside her, shoving Downburst behind him so his massive bulk could provide cover.

Fireballs flew over their heads. Screams and shouts filled the air.

"Oh, no!" Elastigirl heard Apogee cry out. "All this ZAP *over*enhanced my powers!"

Elastigirl kept her body flat on the ground as she lifted her head to see if the coast was clear.

Whoa. Small fires burned across the area where Apogee's uncontrollable blasts had set things aflame. She pulled herself up off the ground, trying to come up with a plan.

Universal Man was inside the netting, shouting at Blazestone. "You were always a terrible partner! I knew you would never make it as a true Super!"

Blazestone laughed. "Oh, please. You're the

one who's not a true Super. I carried you the whole time we were partners."

Universal Man glared at her. "I'm getting out of here now. And I'm coming after *you*!"

Elastigirl saw his eyes narrow with concentration. He flickered and began to use his ability to shift from a full solid to a more gaseous form. "He's going to get through the holes in the net!" Elastigirl realized. "Great! Come on, let's give him backup." She pulled herself up off the ground.

But something was wrong. Universal Man's body was a bubble of shifting molecules that was starting to flow through a hole in the netting, yet his head was still completely solid!

His expression transformed from fury to fear. "The ZAP!"

"Stop!" Elastigirl called. "If your head comes into contact with that much ZAP, who knows—"

Blazestone cackled. "I always said you were full of hot air! And now, you old windbag, it's going to be the end of you!"

"Help!" he cried. "The ZAP is pulling me toward it!"

Several Supers grabbed his still-solid head and

tugged. Elastigirl winced. That must have hurt. But it did the trick. Pulled free of the netting, he was able to rematerialize his body.

"You're going to pay for this, Blazestone," Universal Man hissed.

"I don't think so," Blazestone scoffed. "I think this is one giant gift, no payment required."

"We can't just stand here trying to come up with a perfect plan," Mr. Incredible said. "It's time for action!"

Elastigirl knew he was right. She scanned the area, looking for ideas, for help, for something that would give them the upper hand. She remembered how she had thought Blazestone's arrogance would be her downfall. Now was the time to prove it.

They needed to work together—even if that meant splitting up.

Her eyes landed on a bicycle leaning against the fence that separated that section of the pier into a private area intended for the costume contestants and Supers. She pointed to it. "Is that one of yours?" she asked Downburst.

"Yeah," Downburst said. "I made it specially for

you as a surprise. It stretches. But it hasn't been properly tested yet and I don't know how the ZAP might affect it."

"Time to find out. I'm taking it for a test ride."

"What is she up to?" Mr. Incredible wondered, peering up at Blazestone, who was now hovering above the ground. "And what are *they* doing?"

Blazestone's criminal helpers had rushed to the net and were locking it to the bottom of the band shell. They wore special gloves to protect them from the ZAP.

"Too bad we don't have those gloves," Downburst said.

"We'll just have to make do with what we've got!" Elastigirl said—which, at the moment, didn't seem like much.

"Look!" Apogee shouted and pointed up.

Everyone watched, stunned, as Blazestone used her power to raise herself high into the air. With a furious laugh, she grabbed the top of the net and began to slowly lift the Super-filled band shell off the ground. Elastigirl was thankful the cops had managed to clear the area of civilians. Otherwise, they'd have been in grave danger.

Instead, it was only the Supers who were in real trouble.

"You use your stretch—I'll use my strength," Mr. Incredible said to Elastigirl.

"What will I use?" Downburst worried.

Mr. Incredible clamped a hand on his shoulder. "Everything you've got, kid."

"I'm heading for the bike," Elastigirl said.

"Maybe I can manipulate the locks to release the netting," Downburst said.

"Go for it," Mr. Incredible said. "And I'll go after the criminals!"

"We've got this!" Elastigirl put out her hand. Downburst laid his on top of hers, and then Mr. Incredible placed his hand on top. Elastigirl looked from one to the other, feeling a powerful connection among the three of them. Her mouth twisted up into a crooked grin. She met Mr. Incredible's bright eyes, gleaming with excitement. Downburst's face was a study in determination. She gave a slight nod.

"We've got this!" they shouted together, then flung up their hands.

They raced toward the band shell. Elastigirl

veered off and ran to the fence, dodging wayward blasts and explosions caused by the short-circuiting Super powers. She could hear the Supers yelling at Blazestone above them as she *r-e-a-c-h-e-d* out and grabbed the prototype bike, tugging hard on the handlebars to yank it to her. She flung herself onto the seat and pedaled furiously. She wished she'd asked Downburst how it worked. But that would have taken time. Time they didn't have. She'd just have to consider this on-the-job training!

Blazestone seemed to be struggling a bit with the weight of the Super-filled band shell. It was rising very slowly. Elastigirl wondered where she planned to take it. Or maybe she just meant to keep it up there until the high volume of the ZAP did terrible things to the Supers, short-circuiting their powers.

The bottom of the band shell swayed above Elastigirl. She could see the air in front of Downburst shimmering. He was trying to break the locks without having to touch the radioactive metal. She wasn't sure if the reason it wasn't working was because of the ZAP.

Meanwhile, it seemed Mr. Incredible had already taken out three criminals. They were tied to a tree, moaning. *That guy can really get down to business,* Elastigirl thought.

Elastigirl looked down at the bike gears. "Gotta try something!" She pushed on the red lever. The wheels began to stretch! "Bingo!" she cheered.

She gave herself enough momentum to yank the bike up onto its back wheel and plant the now-oversized front tire onto the slowly rising net. It reached!

"Look! It's Elastigirl," Apogee cried out.

Elastigirl pedaled furiously until the bike was positioned precariously on the netting at the top of the band shell. The stretchy material Downburst had created was also sticky, which helped keep the bike on the net despite the repellent properties of the ZAP.

Elastigirl wrinkled her nose. *What is that awful stink?* She looked down. The ZAP was melting the wheels of the bike! She pedaled harder. As long as she kept moving, she could keep the ZAP from destroying the bike too quickly.

She hoped.

She rode around and around the dome of the netted band shell, trying to come up with an idea. She knew she had to keep up her momentum to avoid falling off—or melting.

"Elastigirl!" someone inside the net cheered.

"You have a plan?" another trapped Super asked hopefully.

"Coming up with one now," Elastigirl responded. Her brow furrowed as she pedaled, trying to think of a way to free the Supers. Contact with the net was highly dangerous, and it seemed pretty indestructible based on how it made everyone's powers so wonky.

Elastigirl peered up at Blazestone. She appeared to be concentrating on guiding the netted band shell out over the water. Trapped inside, the Supers might all drown if she dropped them into the river!

We have to end this, and fast! Elastigirl thought. "Anyone's powers work normally?" she called down into the netted band shell. She had to keep moving, though, so she wasn't sure what the answers were. And her wheels were still melting, not to mention positioned awkwardly on the moving structure. She stretched them again, bringing her seat up higher and farther away from the ZAP. After a full circuit she was above Frozone again.

"E-girl!" Frozone called. "I've been icing the net, but every time I get a section frozen, Blazestone heats it up and it goes back to being all ZAP-py."

"I'll distract her! That may give you time to get to work."

"I'll help!" Apogee said. "But you're going to need to watch out for any ricochets from my blasts."

Elastigirl watched Apogee's head whip back and forth. She spotted Universal Man. "Lift me up!" she ordered the towering Super.

"But–"

"Come on!" Apogee insisted. "You're the tallest Super in here! You want to stop Blazestone, don't you?"

Hearing Blazestone's name, Universal Man immediately gripped Apogee's outstretched hands and yanked her up to a sitting position on his shoulders. Blazestone was still high above them, but Elastigirl knew Apogee's solar-powered energy blast had a pretty long range, even without the ZAP enhancing it.

With Apogee now in place, Elastigirl rode the stretchy bike up to the top, where Blazestone grasped the net.

"Give up now, Blazestone!" Elastigirl shouted.

Blazestone glared at her. "You have *got* to be kidding. What are you going to do? On a melting bicycle? Surrounded by radioactive material?"

Suddenly, a blast startled them both. *The ZAP may increase Apogee's firepower, but it messes with her aim,* Elastigirl realized. *She missed Blazestone by a mile. And she missed me, too, thank goodness.*

"It's over, Blazestone," Apogee called from atop Universal Man's shoulders.

"You got that right!" Blazestone said. "Over for *you!*"

She released one hand from the netting, making it tilt. All the Supers inside tumbled as Blazestone threw pyrotechnic fire first at Apogee and then at Elastigirl. Apogee deflected the crackling and sparking blasts with shots of her own as

Universal Man struggled to stay upright, but one of Apogee's solar flares caught Elastigirl's bike.

"Don't come into contact with the ZAP!" Frozone shouted from below. "You don't know what it's going to do to you!"

Elastigirl looked down. Frozone had iced half the netting! The plan to keep Blazestone occupied was working. One problem: her bike was only about five inches high now—and the handlebars were on fire.

"You can do it!" a young girl called up to her. Elastigirl peered down and saw the young fan in the Elastigirl costume still standing in the back row of the bleachers. "We believe in you."

Elastigirl's heart swelled. And she knew she had only one option.

With a shout, she stretched all her limbs and grabbed hold of Blazestone. The bike fell to the ground and exploded. *Darn.* And just when she was getting the hang of how to use it.

"Get off me!" Blazestone shrieked.

Elastigirl wrapped her legs around Blazestone's torso, twisting to avoid her blasts. She wrapped a super-stretched arm around and around the traitorous villain's throwing arm.

"Let me go!" Blazestone screamed.

"No way," Elastigirl said. "You have two choices. You can let go of the netting to fight me, or you can just give up now."

With a howl of fury, Blazestone released the netting. But as she reared back her arm to charge her firepower, Elastigirl wrapped her other arm around it. She knotted her own arms behind Blazestone's back as an extra precaution.

Elastigirl heard shouts and screams as the band shell crashed back to the ground. Blazestone slumped in her arms. That told Elastigirl Blazestone had realized she'd been defeated.

"I suggest you bring us down nice and gentle," Elastigirl said to Blazestone.

"I don't get you, Elastigirl," Blazestone said as she flew them slowly toward the ground. "I thought we were alike: Strong. Independent."

Elastigirl unwrapped her legs and stretched them the rest of the way down.

"You're right about that," Elastigirl said as she placed her feet back on the ground. "But you forgot about being loyal. And law-abiding. And wanting to make Municiberg a safe and happy place. Those things aren't mutually exclusive."

"Such a Goody Two-shoes," Blazestone sneered.

"Nothing wrong with being good," Elastigirl said. "And I think you're about to discover that it's not such a great idea to be bad!"

Mr. Incredible and Downburst raced over. "We've got all of her henchmen and women in custody," Mr. Incredible announced while Downburst worked to catch his breath. "NSA reinforcements are on the way to deal with Blazestone and any injured Supers."

"Good. I'll be glad when I can get far away from this traitor!" Elastigirl knew she couldn't untie her arms until Blazestone had truly been neutralized. "How are we on getting everyone out of that thing and away from the ZAP?" she asked.

"See for yourself," Mr. Incredible said.

Frozone had managed to freeze the entire net. "I think this will counteract the ZAP's effects," he said.

"Let me test it out," Apogee offered. "If my

powers aren't enhanced anymore, we're good to go."

Apogee stepped up to the netting. She took a deep breath, and Elastigirl took one, too. She really hoped Frozone's freezing had neutralized the ZAP.

Apogee gripped the frozen netting. Then she took a step back and sent out a blast. It tore a hole in the netting.

"Totally normal!" Apogee announced.

The whole group cheered.

"But I wouldn't want to risk using my power to break us out of here," Apogee warned. "We're too close together."

"I got this." Mr. Incredible smashed the icicles the netting had become and released everyone.

Elastigirl continued to grip Blazestone tightly. She stood with Downburst, watching the Supers climb out of their bizarre prison. Some straightened their Supersuits and checked for damage; some hugged. Elastigirl heard a few apologies for short tempers while trapped, and more than one nervous joke was told to break the tension they were all still feeling.

"We did it!" Downburst exclaimed.

"Yup! The Supers have prevailed," Elastigirl said proudly. "We all worked together, as a team."

"Oh, shut up," Blazestone grumbled. "All this togetherness is making me sick."

Downburst glared at her. "I'm embarrassed I ever liked you."

The NSA crime van drove up. Several security officers piled out and ran to free Rick Dicker, Shirley, and the mayor.

Shirley straightened her gold lamé skirt and sequined top with great dignity, then gently dusted off a very large hat that had been knocked to the ground. She placed it carefully on her head, then retrieved Dicker's clipboard from where it had been dropped and handed it to him. Dicker and the officers quickly strode to Elastigirl and Blazestone, while Shirley and the mayor were led into the bleachers to recover after the harrowing ordeal. First aid workers handed them cups of water and waited to see if any of the Supers needed help.

"We can take it from here," Dicker said. The security guards immediately shoved enormous padded gloves onto Blazestone's hands. "That'll prevent blasting," Dicker explained. Elastigirl untangled her stretched arms and released Blazestone. Then she brought her limbs back to their regular lengths.

A furious Universal Man stomped toward them, obviously ready to go ballistic on Blazestone. One of the security officers stepped between him and the traitorous Super. She held her head up defiantly, despite the handcuffs and defeat.

Whatever the security officer whispered in Universal Man's ear, it seemed to satisfy the glowering Super. He gave Blazestone a final scowl, then went to join the group of celebrating Supers.

"Wonder what that guy said to Universal Man," Downburst said.

"Probably just reminded him to let the law do its job," Elastigirl said. "After all, Universal Man is keen on sticking to the rules."

"Sounds right," Downburst said.

The security officers hauled Blazestone into the van. Mr. Incredible joined Elastigirl, Downburst, and Rick Dicker.

"How did this happen?" Dicker asked.

"Blazestone wasn't capturing the bad guys," Elastigirl told him. "She'd been recruiting them.

Every time she ran into a criminal, she only pretended to capture them. Instead, she was bringing them together to make a plan. Then she helped them escape custody."

"Ingenious," Dicker said. He eyed the damaged band shell, and then his gaze roamed to the smoldering pier. "That's a fair amount of damage," he said.

"Small price to pay for saving the Supers," Mr. Incredible said.

"And the citizens of Municiberg," Elastigirl added.

"With no loss of life," Dicker said with pride. "Well done!"

Elastigirl glanced at her fellow Supers and saw the same look of pride on their faces.

"Sorry I destroyed your prototype," Elastigirl told Downburst.

"Oh, that's fine. It was so cool to see it in action," he gushed. "And to think–it was part of how we Supers saved the day!"

Mr. Incredible slung his arms across Elastigirl's and Downburst's shoulders. "We sure did!" he declared.

CHAPTER 13

The mayor of Municiberg and several assistants swarmed around Rick Dicker. "Is there any chance we can salvage Supers Appreciation Day?" the mayor asked. He blotted his sweating forehead with a handkerchief. "This has turned into a public relations nightmare."

"You're worried about PR?" Elastigirl asked. She gestured toward the group of just-freed Supers. "You would have had more than a PR problem on your hands if Blazestone had—"

Rick Dicker held up a hand to cut her off. "Good public relations helps us *all*," he said.

Elastigirl was about to respond when the little girl in the Elastigirl costume ran up to her. She threw her arms around Elastigirl's knees and hugged them. Then she grinned up at the Super.

"I knew you could do it!" the little girl exclaimed. "The grown-ups were nervous, but I was sure you would take care of us!"

Elastigirl knelt down and gave the girl a squeeze. "You cheering me on gave me just the boost I needed," she told the young fan.

Maybe Dicker and the mayor are right, she thought as she stood. She watched the little girl run off to her parents. They definitely looked like they'd been awfully frightened by what had transpired. It would be important to regain the public's trust after Blazestone's betrayal.

"We never did get around to the awards ceremony, did we?" Mr. Incredible asked.

"No," the mayor confirmed. "We *could* do that now. . . ."

"Uh, hate to point out the obvious," Elastigirl said, "but we've kind of lost the venue, not to mention the audience." She pointed to the damaged band shell, no longer in its proper position on the pier, and then to the empty bleachers.

"We just need to let the fans know that they're safe again and that the Supers are all okay," Mr.

Incredible said. "We can announce that everyone should come back to the bleachers if they would like to."

The mayor snapped his fingers and the assistants perked up, looking ready for action. "We'll make a citywide announcement right now—that the awards ceremony is going on as planned!" The assistants scattered.

"Great!" Downburst cheered.

A moment later, vans equipped with megaphones were driving through Municiberg, announcing the all clear and inviting everyone to return to the bleachers for the awards ceremony. Free ice cream was promised to all.

Rick Dicker looked down at his clipboard. "One problem. Blazestone was set to win the Most Criminals Caught award."

"And she wasn't exactly catching them," Elastigirl said.

"Not to mention that she betrayed the NSA," Downburst added. "And all the Supers."

"I wish you *wouldn't* mention it, actually," Dicker said.

Elastigirl wondered if Dicker would get into

trouble. After all, it had been his idea to try to rehabilitate Blazestone by bringing her into the agency.

"So under the circumstances, our winner is disqualified," Dicker said.

"Just give the award to the person with the next highest number," Mr. Incredible suggested.

"Let's see. . . ." Dicker flipped a few pages on the clipboard. "Ah. Well, it's a tie. Between Elastigirl and Mr. Incredible."

Mr. Incredible and Elastigirl gaped at each other.

"That's so cool!" Downburst exclaimed.

Mr. Incredible turned to Dicker. "Well, I for one don't plan to accept it."

"What?" Elastigirl couldn't believe what she was hearing. Up until now he had seemed all about winning.

"Excuse me?" Dicker said.

Mr. Incredible clapped Downburst on the back. "Not unless you include this fella right here. We never could have stopped Blazestone without him."

Downburst's mouth dropped open. "B-b-but... I mean... Huh?"

"You okay with that?" Mr. Incredible asked Elastigirl.

Elastigirl smiled warmly at Mr. Incredible. What a sweet gesture. "You bet I am," she said. She was touched by how kind the more experienced Super was being to the less-than-secure Downburst. It reminded her of how thoughtful that Bob Parr guy had been to the little old lady at the grocery store and to Wendy, the librarian's daughter.

"If that's how you want it," Dicker said, "then that's how it will be."

Downburst beamed. "You mean it?" His dimples were on full display.

"Of course!" Elastigirl told him. "Why, if it wasn't for that bike of yours..."

"Ah, yes. The bicycle." Rick Dicker stroked his chin thoughtfully. "You know, I think I've got a perfect new assignment for Downburst. I'd like you to create some kind of motorized transportation custom-built expressly for Elastigirl."

"That would be great!" Elastigirl said.

"We'll call it the Elasticycle!" Downburst exclaimed. He shook his head as if he couldn't quite believe everything that was happening. "This is the best day ever!"

"It turned out that way," Mr. Incredible said. "Not that I was ever worried," he added with a wink to Elastigirl. She grinned back.

Rick Dicker left them so he could make arrangements for the revamped awards ceremony. Fans were starting to trickle back into the area.

Downburst put his hand on Elastigirl's arm. "I just want to thank you," Downburst told her. "Your belief in me, in my bikes, including me when we patrolled, well . . . it all gave me so much more confidence. It meant a lot to me. I thought you should know that."

Elastigirl felt herself getting a little choked up. *Wow,* she thought. *Being appreciated is pretty amazing*. That's when it hit her. It wasn't about having a big ego or winning awards just for the sake of winning. It was about being proud of what you did, of doing your best, and being able to own your good work. If that meant letting people express their gratitude, then Elastigirl would try to get used to it. There was nothing wrong with knowing you had a skill, that you were special, and that you had something amazing to offer. *Nothing wrong at all,* she thought with pride. She felt a few inches taller—without even stretching.

Apogee strode over. "Glad my powers are back to normal," she said when she joined them. "Maybe you're right," she told Mr. Incredible. "I think from now on I'm going to leave my powers well enough alone. At least until the NSA has done a whole lot more testing!"

"Smart," Mr. Incredible said.

"And big kudos for figuring out what was going on," Apogee told Elastigirl. "Blazestone sure had us fooled."

"We thought it was you at first," Downburst blurted.

For a moment there was silence as Mr. Incredible, Downburst, and Elastigirl waited to see how Apogee would react. Then she burst out laughing.

"Oh, that's rich," she said. She laughed so hard she had to wipe her eyes. "Well, I'm glad you think I'm smart enough to be a criminal mastermind.

And actually, I have to confess," she added with a sly smile, "I was worried it might be one of you three!"

They all looked at one another, eyes wide, then laughed together.

"So, our girls' night at the movies was cut short," Apogee said to Elastigirl. "Wanna try again sometime?"

"I'd like that," Elastigirl said.

"Great," Apogee said. "Now I better head up there. I promised Dicker I'd help present the award. And congratulations, you guys."

Elastigirl watched Apogee saunter away, chatting with the various Supers who were assembling in the bleachers with the fans.

"You know," Elastigirl said, "now I'm kind of sorry I missed the Supers Appreciation Day events. I bet it was fun. For the citizens *and* the Supers." She recalled Bob Parr's words when they'd discussed the event at the grocery store. "Everyone needs a little appreciation now and then."

"I suppose," Mr. Incredible said. "But shouldn't we be out fighting crime? Not spending our time posing for photos and autographs."

From what she'd seen from Mr. Incredible before today, that was a surprising position for him to take. Could she have been wrong about him? He did keep proving to be a much more thoughtful guy than she'd first believed. He wasn't all ego all the time. "But without the goodwill of the public, we could have a harder time fighting crime," she countered.

Mr. Incredible opened his mouth to respond, but instead of saying anything, he just cocked his head and stared at Elastigirl. An idea was obviously forming. Then: "H-Helen . . . ?" he asked tentatively.

Elastigirl's jaw dropped. "Bob??"

They burst out laughing.

"Who?" Downburst asked.

Mr. Incredible and Elastigirl were laughing so hard they couldn't speak. Elastigirl doubled over guffawing while Mr. Incredible hooted and slapped his thigh.

"Looks like the party is over here," Frozone said as he joined them. "What's got them in hysterics?" he asked Downburst.

"I don't know," Downburst replied.

Elastigirl struggled to get her laughter under control. "It's a long story."

"Yeah . . ." Mr. Incredible said. "You kinda had to be there."

"Spend much time at the library?" Elastigirl asked.

"I'm glad your face didn't get stuck that way," Mr. Incredible teased.

That set them off again.

Frozone shook his head. "Well, when you've got your senses back, Mr. I, I want to discuss that terrible cartoon with you."

"Terrible?" Elastigirl asked, catching her breath.

"Aww, it wasn't *that* bad," Mr. Incredible argued. "Frozone had some . . . *artistic differences* with how his character was portrayed," he explained to Elastigirl and Downburst.

"Not just mine!" Frozone protested. "They had us crime-fighting with a bunny. Can you believe that? A *bunny*!" He threw up his hands, making tiny snowflakes drift onto their heads.

"Don't get all iced out," Mr. Incredible said. "I already spoke to Dicker about your objections. They're going to shelve the cartoon for now."

"That's too bad," Elastigirl said. "I'd have loved to have seen *that*!" She gazed up at Mr. Incredible. *First impressions can be so wrong,* she thought. He was much nicer than she had first believed. And they actually had more in common than she realized.

Hmmmm.

"In fact," she said, before she could talk herself out of it, "if you can arrange it, I'd love to go to a screening of it with you."

She wasn't going to rush into anything, but hey, maybe one date wouldn't hurt.

Mr. Incredible studied her a moment. "You mean, like a date?"

"Yeah. Exactly like a date," Elastigirl replied.

"You got it." Mr. Incredible grinned.

"Awwwww," Frozone said, slinging an arm over each of their shoulders. "My two best friends!"

"Rick Dicker is waving us over," Downburst said. "It must be time for the awards ceremony."

"I'll go grab a seat," Frozone said. "See you guys later!"

Downburst, Mr. Incredible, and Elastigirl headed toward Rick Dicker and his assistant.

Shirley's shiny gold skirt combined with the silver sequined blouse made Elastigirl squint in the bright sunlight. That feathered hat must be what she wore for special occasions, Elastigirl observed.

They reached Dicker. "Okay, we can't use the damaged band shell," he informed them, "so you'll just accept your shared award right in front of the bleachers. Apogee and I will announce it. Shirley will show you where to wait."

"Great!" Downburst said. He and Mr. Incredible followed Shirley, but Dicker took Elastigirl's arm, holding her back.

"After the great work you did today, the NSA has asked me to once again offer you a team leadership." Before Elastigirl could respond, he held up his hand. "And you could pick your own team members."

Elastigirl took in a deep breath. This was a little different from being handed a problematic pair of bickering Supers like Universal Man and Blazestone. Still . . .

She shook her head. "It's an honor, and I appreciate the recognition," she told him. "But I just want to stay unaffiliated." This time she held up her hand to stop *him* from speaking. “At least for now,” she added with a grin.

She strode over to Mr. Incredible and Downburst, who were waiting at the edge of the bleachers.

“You know, I still don’t want to lead a team,” Elastigirl told them. “And I do value my independence. But I learned something today.”

“Yeah?” Mr. Incredible said. “What was that?”

“We really can be greater than the sum of our parts,” she said.

“What do you mean?” Downburst asked.

“Being a good team member is another Super skill to master,” Elastigirl said. “And I know exactly what I’m going to say in my award acceptance speech.” Elastigirl grinned at her two new friends. “When it comes to teamwork and being appreciated, maybe I do need to be a little more . . . flexible.”

The End